View of Dawn in the Tropics

ff

VIEW OF DAWN IN THE TROPICS

G. Cabrera Infante

Translated from the Spanish
by Suzanne Jill Levine
Revised by the author

faber and faber
LONDON · BOSTON

First published in Great Britain in 1988
by Faber and Faber Limited
3 Queen Square London WC1N 3AU

Originally published in Spanish in 1974
as *Vista del amanecer en el tropico*

Printed in Great Britain by
Mackays of Chatham PLC, Chatham, Kent
All rights reserved

British Library Cataloguing in Publication Data

Cabrera Infante, G.
View of dawn in the tropics.
I. Title II. Vista del amanecer en
el tropico. *English*
836[F]   PQ7389.c233

ISBN 0-571-15186-8

To the memory of
Comandante Plinio Prieto, who was shot
by firing squad
in September 1960

In memory of
Comandante Alberto Mora,
who shot himself
in September 1972

Si amanece, nos vamos.

Goya, *Los Caprichos*

THE ISLAND CAME OUT OF THE SEA like a Venus land: out of the foam constantly beautiful. But there were more islands. In the beginning they were solitary isles really. Then the isles turned into mountains and the shallows in between became valleys. Later the islands joined to form a bigger island which soon was green where it wasn't reddish or brown. The island under the tropic of Cancer was a haven for birds and for fish but it never was good for mammals. The island was actually an archipelago: a longer island near a round smaller island surrounded by thousands of islets and isles and even other islands that later were called keys to the ocean and the sea. Since the long and narrow island had a defined form (curiously that of a cayman) it devoured the group geographically and nobody saw the archipelago. It is still there but the natives prefer to call the island the Island and they forget all about the thousand keys, isles and islets that glut the passage around the big island like clots in a green wound that never heals.

There's the island, still coming out between the sea and the gulf, garlanded by keys and cays and fastened by the stream to the ocean. There it is . . .

. . . history begins with
the arrival of the white man,
whose deeds it records.

Fernando Portuondo

BUT BEFORE THE WHITE MAN WERE THE INDIANS. The first
to arrive – they came, like all of them, from the continent
– were the Ciboneys. Then came the Tainos, who treated
the Ciboneys like servants. The Ciboneys didn't know
how to till the earth or make utensils; they were still in
the gathering stage when the Tainos arrived. In turn the
Tainos and the Ciboneys were at the mercy of the Caribs,
cannibal warriors, who were constantly raiding the eastern
part of the island. The Caribs were fierce and proud and
had a motto: '*Ana carina roto*' – 'Only we are people'.

When the white men arrived they marvelled at the sight
of the island: 'More beautiful than any I have seen, filled
with trees, verdant and luxuriant, all along the river . . .'
Some explorers sent to reconnoitre the surroundings
returned with praises for the hospitality of the aborigines,
many of whom 'carry a burning wood in their hands, with
certain herbs to fume'. There was 'a varietie of birds' and
'a great varietie of trees, herbs and fragrant flowers' and
'dogs that do not bark'. The natives went around half
naked, both men and women, and they were very unsus-
pecting. They had, besides, the dreadful habit of bathing
so much that when the king was informed, he issued a
royal decree recommending that they not bathe too much,
since 'we believe that it could do you much harm'.

When the discoverers arrived, there were more than one
hundred thousand Indians on the island. A hundred years

later there weren't even five thousand. They had been decimated by measles, smallpox, influenza and bad treatment, in addition to suicide, which they began committing in great numbers. On the other hand, there were battles between the Indians, armed only with bows and arrows, and the visitors, who rode armoured horses and wore armour, thus becoming truly ironclad machines. The natives, in turn, lavished upon the conquistadores two plagues: the vice of smoking and syphilis, which was endemic among them.

In the beginning the rebel natives had some success, being favoured by the rough and familiar terrain. But they were finally overcome by the sword and the horse.

IN THE ENGRAVING YOU CAN SEE THE EXECUTION, or rather the torture, of an Indian chief. He's tied to a stake on the right. Flames are already beginning to cover the straw at the foot of the stake. A Franciscan priest, with his shovel hat hanging down his back, approaches him. He has a book – a missal or a Bible – in one hand and in the other he bears a crucifix. The priest approaches the Indian somewhat fearfully, since a bound Indian is always more frightening than a free one – perhaps because he can break loose. He is still trying to convert him to the Christian faith. On the left of the engraving there's a group of conquistadores in iron armour, with muskets in their hands and unsheathed swords, watching the execution. In the centre of the engraving is a man meticulously occupied in bringing the torch close to the Indian. The smoke from the blazing fire fills the whole upper right side of the engraving and you can no longer see anything there. But in the background, on the left, you can see several conquistadores on horseback, pursuing a half-naked crowd of Indians who flee rapidly towards the edges of the engraving.

The legend says that the priest came close to the Indian and suggested that he go to heaven. The Indian chief knew little Spanish but understood enough to ask: 'And the Spaniards, they also go to heaven?' 'Yes, my son,' said the good father from amid the bitter smoke and the heat. 'Good Spaniards also go to heaven,' said in a paternal and kindly tone. Then the Indian raised his proud chieftain's head, with long, greasy hair tied behind his ears and the aquiline profile still visible on the beer-bottle labels that bear his name, and he said calmly, speaking from amid the flames: 'Better I not go to heaven, better I go to hell.'

UPON REACHING A LARGE VILLAGE, the conquistadores found some two hundred thousand Indians gathered in the central square, awaiting them with gifts – a quantity of fish and also cassava bread – all of them squatting and some smoking. The Indians began to hand out the food, when a soldier took out his sword and attacked one of them, lopping off his head in one stroke. Other soldiers imitated the action of the first and without any provocation began to slash with their swords left and right. There was even greater butchery when several soldiers entered a *batey*, a very large house in which over five hundred Indians had gathered, 'among whom few had the chance to escape'. A witness tells us: 'There was a stream of blood as if many cows had been slaughtered.' When an inquest into the bloody incident was ordered, it was found out that the conquistadores, upon receiving such a friendly reception, 'thought that so much courtesy was intended to kill them for sure'.

IN WHAT OTHER COUNTRY OF THE WORLD is there a province named Matanzas, meaning 'Slaughter'?

A MAGNIFICENT MACHINE WAS INVENTED to track down and destroy escaped Indians and runaway slaves: the killer bloodhound. Its fame spread throughout the territory and very soon many were exported to the United States' southern regions, where they were known as Cuban hounds.

IN ANOTHER ENGRAVING YOU CAN SEE AN ESCAPED SLAVE, cornered by two bloodhounds. Barefoot, in threadbare clothes, the runaway clutches a long knife or machete. One of the dogs draws dangerously near his left, while the other closes in on his right. In the middle of the engraving there's an earthen cooking pot and a low flame. You can also see a palm-leaf or straw hat. Between the fugitive and the dogs there's only the space of the knife cleaving the air. The caption says: 'The runaway slave, caught by the dogs, defends himself from them like a cornered beast.'

THE TOBACCO PLANTERS, ALL WHITE, HAD RISEN IN PROTEST against the monopoly decreed by the government. Not all of them were in the uprising, but those who weren't saw their crops destroyed by the mutineers. Now they were a mob of eight or nine hundred men, who threatened to march on the capital. But the alerted captain-general sent a troop of two hundred well-armed men to meet the planters. The troops waited in ambush and when the mutineers appeared, they fired upon them, killing many and capturing the rest. Of the wounded, eight died and the eleven of the advance guard who had been captured were executed, without a trial and by order of the captain-general, and their corpses hung 'from different trees on the main thoroughfares as a public warning'.

HERE'S A MAP MADE A FEW DAYS (or maybe weeks or months) before the English attacked the capital of the island. As you can see, the map is a rather rough sketch, but it accomplishes its purpose. It indicates with precision the Morro fortress across the bay, and those other forts in Havana proper: La Punta, Atarés Castle and the San Lázaro Tower. You may observe how the map distorts the characteristics of the city itself and its environs. It is believed that the map was made by an English spy.

THE CITY WAS UNDER SIEGE for more than a month and a half. Finally the English managed to dynamite a passage behind the Morro fortress and enter through there. Before the attack, the earl in command of the English forces sent a message to the commander of the fort demanding his surrender. But the commander refused to surrender, announcing that he would fight to the finish. The English troops entered the Morro and found almost no resistance, since most of the defenders surrendered or fled toward the city. During the attack the commander of the fort was mortally wounded, falling with his sword in his hand. This show of courage to the enemy was admired by the English, who ordered that he be carried to the city to be tended by physicians. When the commander died, the English joined in the mourning, firing their rifles into the air as a last salute.

IN ANOTHER ENGRAVING YOU CAN SEE A CHAIN GANG OF SLAVES. They are led, four abreast, by one slave-driver at the head of the line, and another spurring them on with a whip. The slaves are joined by a clamp, usually made of wood. They are barefoot and half naked, while the slave-drivers wear sombreros to protect them from the sun. One of the slave-drivers smokes a cigar and doesn't seem to be in a hurry to take his gang to its destination, while the other snaps the whip in the air. Behind the group you can see a palm tree and several banana trees, which give the rest of the engraving an exotic, almost bucolic touch.

HISTORY SAYS: 'The coloured people began to nurture among themselves the goal of imitating the Haitians. The insurrections of the blacks in the sugar mills were more and more frequent, but they lacked unity and leadership.'

Legend has it that the largest uprising was crushed in time because the governor himself found out about it when, during his rounds, he heard some blacks talking in a hut outside the town walls.

In reality, as often happens, the conspirators were betrayed by a neighbour who lived in the house on whose roof the conspirators used to meet.

All the conspirators were hanged.

HE WAS A POET and the son of a Spanish dancer and a mulatto and he had to earn his living as a comb-maker. He had some talent and his poems began to be known and appreciated on the island. But he longed to be known outside.

His life was marked by misfortunes. When he was born they deposited him at the orphanage, and when he was barely thirty-five he was apprehended, accused of conspiring against the colonial powers and sentenced to be shot. During the trial, in which they couldn't prove him guilty of any crime, he remained serene. He spent the night before the execution writing a prayer in the form of a poem. With it he achieved posthumous fame abroad.

THE GRAFFITO, still so touching after one hundred and fifty years, says:

> Long live the Yndepence
> through Reafon orForce
> Senor citie hall of Trinidad
> yndependence ordeath

HIS LIFE WAS MARKED BY CONTRADICTIONS. He was born in Venezuela, and still very young, he joined the Spanish army and fought against the liberators of his country. He came to the island with the troops defeated in Venezuela. He achieved a colonel's rank and 'was known for his bravery'. He was also known as a sportsman and a man-about-town. He was very good-looking and cut quite a dash in the salons of high society. He finally married a girl from a rich Havana family and was transferred to Spain, then engaged in the Carlist wars. There he was rapidly promoted until he became field marshal. He returned to the island with important commissions. But in some way – perhaps his sporting life was the cause – he began to conspire against the colonial powers of which he was still a part. He had to flee the country.

He returned as the leader of an expedition intended to 'free the country from its colonial yoke'. The campaign was a failure, but for the first time he fought on the island under the banner that, in a distant future, would become the national flag. He again fled abroad, escaping almost miraculously. A short while after, he organized another expedition, which also failed. But this time he was caught, tried and sentenced to die on the gallows. They say that he went up on the scaffold smiling to the crowd that came to attend the execution, with the same elegant smile he had displayed in the city's drawing rooms barely ten years before.

THE LEADER OF THE UPRISING was a lawyer with a degree from Barcelona, a cultivated man who had visited almost all the countries of Europe. He was of medium height but his demeanour made him seem taller. He was also an excellent rider and skilled swordsman. On the day of the insurrection he ordered that all the slaves who worked on his plantation be freed and he drew up a manifesto which began: 'We hold these venerable principles to be sacred: we believe that all men are created equal; we cherish tolerance, order and justice in all spheres: we respect the lives and property of all peace-loving citizens, even the Spaniards themselves, who are residents in this territory; we uphold universal suffrage, which assures the sovereignty of the people . . .'

HE MARCHED AT THE HEAD OF A COLUMN of 'some two hundred men, very few of whom carried firearms', towards the neighbouring town. He assumed he could occupy it without resistance, since there would be no other troops there except some *salvaguardias* from the local vigilante group. 'On the way there they made a short stop at the sugar mill . . . and then at the plantation . . . where they had lunch. They continued the journey in the afternoon, thus arriving . . . at nightfall of the aforementioned Sunday the eleventh . . . As a precaution, the *caudillo* stopped before reaching town and ordered a reconnaissance.' He also sent a surrender order to the regional captain, who 'offered to surrender at his own discretion'.

But at that very moment an enemy column was entering the town from the other side, and when they learned that the rebels were near, they organized an ambush in the square. The rebel column entered the square in darkness, shouting *Viva*, and received an unexpected volley of gunfire which forced them to retreat 'in complete disorder'. But the town became a symbol of the country's fight for freedom.

THE INSURGENTS succeeded in taking an important city and entered it 'in the midst of general patriotic intoxication'.

The bells of several churches rang at the same time, salvoes were fired, horses reared, when, 'at the request of a fiery crowd', Perucho Figueredo, seated on his horse, composed verses to be sung to the rhythm of a march he had also composed, borrowing from Mozart, which they all hummed. The verses began:

> *To battle run, ye men of Bayamo*
> *Our fatherland proudly observes thee.*

But a stanza later it promised:

> *To die for the fatherland*
> *is to live . . .*

A FEW DAYS LATER an enemy column would be defeated by rebels armed only with machetes capable of cutting 'the barrell off a rifle . . . in one blow'. Thus the machete became the favourite weapon of rebels.

The machete is not, like the revolver or the dagger, a defensive or an offensive weapon: it is a work tool, made to cut sugar cane, but also used to clear paths in the jungle. It looks like a cross between a Napoleonic sabre and a medieval sword, and its handle, though usually wooden, may be made of bull's horn and sometimes of expensive mother-of-pearl. The best proudly bear an English trademark which says 'Collins'. The rebels would call it 'coyeens' or 'guaranteed'.

THE ENEMY TROOPS, under the command of a count, could boast of nearly three thousand men, while the rebel column had barely five hundred riflemen. The battle – or rather the massacre – took place by a river that is now a dusty ditch. The result of the battle of machetes against cannon fire was not long in doubt. 'The army of patriots had to retreat in great disarray, and the Spaniards, taking advantage of that moment, hastily buried their corpses and continued their march toward Bayamo, without finding any obstacle there.'

But the rebels decided to burn the city – the first they had taken – before handing it over to the enemy, and when the count entered it he found only ruins, still burning, and ashes, which flew like dust in the wind.

THEY HAD BEEN PLAYING among the graves in the cemetery ('Alas! poor Yorick', etc.) while waiting for the anatomy lecturer to arrive. Afterwards they left the wheelbarrow with the bones in a corner. But the next day it was discovered that the glass on one of the tombs had been scratched, and it wasn't any old tomb: it belonged to a Spanish journalist who had died abroad in a formal duel with an exiled Cuban. Immediately there was a big to-do among the Spanish officials. Fearful of the volunteer corps, they agreed to bring the students to trial, and chose them at random among all the students at the medical school. Some of the chosen had not even gone to lectures that day. Two of them weren't in the city. Finally, eight among them were tried, sentenced to death and shot. Not one of them was older than twenty years.

SERIOUSLY WOUNDED, the former chief of the rebellion stayed behind in the rebel hospital. When he got better he knew that he would be a cripple for life. Nevertheless he decided to stay there. 'Here I will be useful,' he wrote in a letter. When the army moved on to another campaign, he didn't go with them because he had become attached to the region: he liked the strange giant ferns and the classes he'd give to the children in the area, and also his morning excursions to gather wild honeycombs. He also liked to write letters, and every once in a while a courier, whom he taught to read and write, would pass through. 'I'm satisfied with what I have,' he wrote to his wife. 'I live in a hut or in the open air, amid strange arboreous vegetation. I feel strong. I eat what they give me: fruit, and occasionally the meat of yard birds, and *hutias*, and wild pigs.' He was a naïve man and he adorned the mountain with his romantic prose: ' . . . the nightingales sing and charm the vesper and from the peaks there descends a fleeting, gallant little brook'. Despite the pathetic fallacy and even though his hovel had become a hut and the mockingbirds and thrushes evening's nightingales, he also knew how to look at reality. One of the generals met with a foreign journalist at the village and he served as translator, and somehow the enemy learned of his hiding place. The courier came to warn him, but he calmed him down and all he did was to write letters. 'I believe that I will never die a prisoner,' he wrote to his brother, 'since my gun has six bullets, five for the enemy and one for me. After knowing such freedom, I could never live as a prisoner. Between death and prison, I choose death.'

A little boy comes to warn him at dawn that the army is approaching, and he limps out of the village. He hides in the jungle all morning. At noon he feels thirsty and looks for *curujeyes*, the parasite plant, enemy of the tree and friend of the traveller: they are all dry already. He is on his way down the mountain toward the river, when a wandering sentry spots him. He shoots, wounds the sentry and runs toward the stream. He feels a blow in his leg and knows that they got him. He takes shelter among the great white rocks. A soldier is about to jump down on him and he shoots him point blank. The soldier rolls down among the stones and he stands up straight to look at him: it's the first man he's ever killed. And the last: a bullet enters his neck, another his chest, another his stomach. He falls in the water and floats downstream, his body finally resting among the roots.

IN THE ENGRAVING, published in New York, you can see in the foreground four *mambises* – that's what the rebels called their insurgent army to distinguish it from the guerrillas, who were made up of Spaniards or Cuban traitors – three on foot and one on horseback. The rider is black and wears his machete on his belt. Two of the others are also black, and unlike the rider, they're barefoot. One of them is sitting on the right, his head leaning against his rifle. The other black chats with a white *mambí*; he's wearing a kerchief on his head, while all the others wear palm-leaf hats. The white *mambí*'s sword is unsheathed and he holds it nonchalantly in his right hand while with his left he takes the reins of the horse, a *criollo* pony, fourteen hands high. The *mambí* with the pirate-style kerchief on his head sports a rifle with a bayonet. While he chats with the white *mambí* he holds his rifle in front of him, almost at attention. In the background, to the right, you can see two *mambises*, one white and the other black, talking under a palm tree. Further to the right there's a banana– or coconut-tree leaf. On the left, in the foreground, there's a tree which seems to be an *ateje*. Way in the background but in the centre of the engraving you can see a sentry.

DESPITE THE FACT THAT HE WAS VERY ILL, they took him to face the firing squad, not in a carriage but mounted on a donkey. They had to help him down and he was so emaciated that one could barely recognize the lively composer of the march that, a quarter of a century later, would be the national anthem. They almost dragged him to the stone wall.

HE WAS A POET TURNED REVOLUTIONARY and he was on several expeditions which ended in shipwreck. Convinced that one should make peace and not war, he returned to the island with a safe-conduct from the Governor-General. But when he arrived at the insurgents' general head-quarters he didn't say a word. 'He didn't make a move,' the rebel leader later said.

When he returned to the city he was put in prison despite the safe-conduct, and locked up in a cell at the Fortress. He was in prison for several months, silently accused of being a traitor by the rebels, and publicly accused by the enemy as a rebel.

Locked in his cell, he wrote this poem:

> Don't fly, you restless swallow,
> In search of my dark grave.
> Can't you see, swallow?
> Over the poet's resting place
> There is no cypress tree, no weeping willow!

They finally shot him at Lane of Laurels, which was actually a dry moat.

THE TROOPS CALLED THEIR LEADER THE MAJOR out of respect for his character more than as an acknowledgement of rank. One day the Major was out on horseback inspecting the terrain, practically alone, when he was struck down by a bullet. Immediately confusion reigned among his men, who tried to rescue his body. But the enemy fire got thicker and they were forced to abandon the quest.

Later, almost by chance, the enemy found his corpse in the tall grass. When they searched him they realized it was the Major and they quickly transported the corpse to the capital of the province, where it was cremated and the ashes scattered to the wind. They did everything so hastily that it seemed as if they were afraid that even his ashes might rise up in revolt.

THERE WEREN'T EVEN TWO DOZEN: they weren't armed: they had only surprise and courage on their side. They carried sticks and stones and their canteens for drinking or storing water, maybe one shotgun. Naturally they didn't take the garrison. But the attack scattered the regiment and they grabbed some rifles and a lot of ammunition.

The invading column took the fort a week later, and the horses, rebels and dead soldiers, whom their sheltered comrades did not dare come out to bury, were still up there, on the *meseta*. Also, a wounded rebel was up there, who told the story of the attack with tired, hurried words. The general couldn't believe it, but he saw the dead men and animals rotting in the sun, and the tin jugs clanking and shining in the night as if they were bayonets and machetes. Then he spoke to the troops and said that he had seen brave, fearless and even crazed men at war, but that these martyrs (pointing to the dead), and the heroes who came out of the battle alive, were the bravest of the brave. Then someone handed him one of the jugs, which had been pierced by a bullet, and the general, whose beard and hair prevented them from seeing his face clearly, pushed his hat back. In his voice one could hear his emotion and respect when he said, looking at the jug: 'And I called these things impedimenta!'

THE GENERAL HAD SET UP CAMP with a handful of men, when they were caught off guard by the enemy. Ordered to surrender, he decided that suicide was better and he shot himself in the chin. The bullet pierced his mouth and nose and came out at his forehead, where it would soon become a star-shaped scar.

When they informed the general's mother that he had surrendered, she answered that they couldn't mean her son. When they explained that before he was captured by the enemy he had shot himself, she said: 'Ah, that's my son, all right!'

'THE RELAY POSTS were stationed at certain intervals and the couriers were ready at a moment's notice to deliver any dispatch on the double.' This is not a description of the pony express but rather of the rebel mail service.

THE NEPHEW TALKED ABOUT HIS DEAD UNCLE as if talking about a Greek hero. It's true that his uncle was a living legend. But sometimes it seemed he was exaggerating. Like now. Look, he said, they gave it to 'im in the leg and knocked 'im down and he didn't faint or nothin' – I mean, look, he resisted and kept walkin' with his foot. Of course he hadn't taken more than three steps when he fell right there and then. They got 'im in the knee, see, in this bone here, what's it called, so that one was on top of the other, like that, he said, crossing one arm over the other on his chest, and it wouldn't come down. Then we picked 'im up and took 'im into a hut. The hut was bigger than that there tree, so we hung 'im from the ceiling, see, but his feet still hung down to the floor, he was so tall. Then I got up there and hung 'im by the armpits right up there, on the beam, so high up that if I looked down I got dizzy, and then I got down, and hung on to his feet, like this, I grabbed one foot and then the other and I hung from there, like this, real hard, by God, with all my strength, and the bone went back into place. And my uncle, he didn't even make a peep and didn't faint or nothin', because I saw 'im sweatin' and I think he saw me sweatin' 'cause it was so hot inside the hut, all closed in. And what d'you think he said when the bone went back into place and my uncle was still up there on the beam? Hey, he said, nephew, let's see if you can get me down from here – I'm startin' to smell like Christ – just like that, and the God's honest truth, he did look like Christ on the cross hangin' up there, and as he was a-cursin' and a-swearin' and gettin' into a temper, we took 'im down in a jiffy, just like that, he said, and looked at the gathering, and as he saw some people laughing, he said: I swear by my mother may she rest in peace it's the whole truth, he said, nothin' but the truth. There are people here who know it's so because they were around then, he said. The group laughed again and then the colonel stands up in front of the lantern and says with his pipe in his mouth, chewing the mouthpiece or his words: There's a lot of truth in what he says. That's the way his uncle was, he says. A hell of a man, he said, and they stopped laughing.

CONCENTRATION CAMPS WERE INVENTED IN CUBA in 1896 by the then Spanish Governor-General. According to the *Encyclopaedia Britannica*, 'the Madrid Government sent General Valeriano Weyler to Cuba to command the Spanish troops. As part of his efforts to pacify the country, General Weyler instituted his concentration policy.' There was a governmental decree on the island that said: 'All inhabitants of the countryside or outside town walls shall reassemble *within a period of eight days* in the towns occupied by troops. Any individual found in open country after this time will be considered a rebel, and condemned as such.' *Reconcentrados*, as the prisoners were called in Spanish, 'died by the thousands'. They were mostly poor peasants, women and children.

Barbed wire originated in the USA where it is called barb wire. It had been used until this century for fencing in cattle only. The British put barbed wire to a nastier use in South Africa during the Boer War. The age of barbed-wire camps had just begun. The rest, as they say, is history. Comments *Britannica:* 'Barbed-wire machines are all fundamentally alike.'

THE CAMPAIGN DIARY of the nearly bald little man with the big moustache doesn't say what happened at the meeting he and the major-general had with the black general. There has been much conjecture; people have even said that the black general actually slapped the little man in an argument over the military versus the civil command of the insurrection. The fact is that after the war, kind hands tore out the pages of the diary that spoke of the meeting, and thus helped turn the meeting into historic gossip.

The truth is that after the meeting, the little man with the big moustache was elected president of the republic in arms and acclaimed as such by the regiment.

At that point they asked the major-general how the black general could start the invasion with such a small regiment, and the former replied: 'He is taking with him a great army: his own strategy.'

A few days later the little man, whom they all now called the President, and the major-general clashed with an enemy column. No one knows how the events occurred. Some say that the President saw himself surrounded by enemy forces and tried to evade capture. Others say that the President started galloping in the direction of the enemy. Still others speak of a runaway horse. The truth is that he received a bullet in his head, falling from his horse very close to the enemy troops, and it was impossible to recover his body. Recognized by the enemy, he was thrown over the back of a mule and the enemy took him with them as the spoils of war. First they buried him in the countryside. But then they exhumed the corpse and embalmed it to take him to the city for burial. In time this corpse became an enormous load on the country. Converted into a martyr, the little man grew and grew until they finally couldn't stand the weight. But all invoked his name, speaking of an immensely great dead man – though when they buried him he was barely five feet five inches tall.

THE DUST FROM THE ROAD (it's July and there's no rain, and the region is a great dust bowl where the slightest breeze raises clouds of white or red or black dirt that erase the roads, camouflage the houses and paint the trees an unhealthy colour) made his beard grey. But even before he started to walk with his long, quick martial stride, even before he left his horse, they all knew he was the general. Without saluting, he asked for the other general, who was under his command.

He wasn't coming on an inspection visit or to plan an offensive or even to exchange ideas about the next operation. They would perhaps talk (after chatting about fighting cocks and horses and women, in that order because both of them are peasants, after dessert and coffee at dusk) about the state of the war in general or of the country or they would bet on the days left to the regime. He was coming to have lunch, invited to eat a whole cow. A gift from the cattle baron, said the other general, smiling, when he invited him. Always giving us little gifts; looks like he's a rebel too.

He was late, having avoided enemy posts on the way, and it was already two in the afternoon. The captain told him he would find the other general down by the river, where they done roast the cow (that's the way he said it, using rustic phrasing), and he went down to the riverbank, where bamboo and arum and wild watercress grew, and saw a group by the pit that's still burning. The general has yours, General, said one of them, there under that tamarind tree (pointing). He's been waitin' for ya, he began to say, and stopped when he saw the general's stare.

He walked slowly along the shore, enjoying himself in

37

the fresh air, thanking the river for keeping its bed from the sun and the dust when the streams of the region were dry, saying out loud, Thank you, river, taking off his hat, going down to the water, washing his face and beard and hair, saying thanks again, leaving his head wet, his hair loose and dripping.

The other general was way under the tamarind tree. Eating already, he was living up to his fame, devouring an enormous piece of cow, and the general pretended to be surprised, just a bit. You eatin' that all by yourself? he said, and the other general, with his mouth full of meat, the fat dripping from his chin and hands and arms, a wild joy in his eyes, answered from amid the food: No, sir, the sweet potato's washin' it down. The two of them laughed and the other general pointed to his piece of meat, also big, lying on a royal palm leaf, with green plantains and sweet potato on the side. The general sat down on the grass and began to eat hungrily, voraciously, happy about his first meat in two months. The other general went to the river and took out of the water two brown bottles stoppered with wild cork. He displayed them from afar, one in each hand and up high, like two trout. What luxury, said the general. The bottles were sweating and they drank straight from the cold bottles while they ate and talked and laughed. It was like a picnic.

BUT IT WAS NO PICNIC. Scouts brought the news that the column was already in view. They had to either attack or give up and leave a rear guard. The general decided to attack. The advance guard made contact, then they exchanged shots. The bullets buzzed over the rebels and their sound indicated the calibre of the gun, and when to raise their heads.

They were shooting back and forth about ten minutes and the general, tired of the hindrance, ordered them to advance. He stood up and went to the edge of the road. It was a side road, actually a footpath, and on the other side, in the curve, hidden by an embankment, was the enemy. He made the signal to attack and placed himself at the head of the column, as usual.

When they saw him fall, they all believed he had got it in the leg, but the colonel went near him and saw that the general was wounded in the head and in the neck. They also wounded the colonel. Two rebels came and pulled them away from the edge of the road. The doctor crept up on all fours in the crab grass. The colonel had been grazed on the hip, a flesh wound. The general's wounds were fatal. He took a bullet out from under the skin of the skull and said to the third in command that nothing could be done. He pointed to the grey slime that ran down the wounded man's face. A loss of brain matter, he said. He's dying.

They retreated in order, with nine casualties. The colonel, bandaged, remained at the head of the troop and ordered that the dead be buried. Then he called the captain and said something to him in a whisper. They continued the retreat, leaving a rear guard posted.

The burial patrol marched toward three *dagame* trees

which could be seen in a nearby stream and the colonel took charge of burying the rebel general and a corporal on the other side of the hill. In a recognizable place, he said, but without identifying the graves. When they left, he walked back and marked twenty paces between the trees. He had remained with two officers and told them to dig. He searched the general, stripping him of his papers, photographs, money, which he kept, and the watch and the gold chain. He took out of his wallet a coin, an amulet, and put it in a pocket of the dead man's combat jacket. He helped them bury the corpse and upon noticing that the dirt on the grave looked fresh, they threw grass and dry leaves and branches on top. Before returning, he made the officers swear that they didn't know where the general was buried, that they had forgotten and that they wouldn't remember it again until the war was over. His identification is a silver dollar on the skeleton, he said.

THE GENERAL WAS CALLED WAR LIGHTNING by friends and foes. When he led one of his famous cavalry charges, machetes deadlier than any sword, he was always in the front line. Before battle he used to tell his riders, tall in the saddle, shouting, bigger than life: 'Who's ahead of me?' He had been made a general before being thirty during the ten-year war and now he was a three-star general, virtually the general-in-chief. At least everybody thought he was the leader. Courage incarnate, he had won the total devotion of his men. They had even nicknamed him the Titan of Bronze. (Later the equestrian statue of him that was erected in Havana was made of bronze in an eponymous tautology.) It was a well-known fact of war that he had survived twenty-two bullet wounds but he never bragged. He was virtually indestructible and the enemy knew it. No one could say if they were more frightened of the man or of his machete.

His greatest feat, though, was to write a letter to the revolutionary junta, which became his political testament. 'I have an inkling', he wrote, 'that the majority of the people on this island would like to see me elected president as soon as independence is won. I would never allow this to happen, for reasons I must keep not in my mind but in my heart.' The reasons he alluded to were that the general was black. He finished his letter with a personal remark like a flourish of his pen: 'I had rather dream now of a trip abroad with my men, to spare the fatherland any conflicts when freedom comes.' The trip he had in mind was an old wish of his: the black general wanted to see Paris before he died. More than once he had cheered up his war-weary officers by telling them all about a Paris

41

he had never visited. He always called the city, rather endearingly, *la ville Lumière*.

THE OLD GENERAL WITH THE STAR ON HIS FOREHEAD was sitting in his hammock under a *guásima* and a carob tree, dictating a letter. He was informing their delegate in New York about the war, and ended with a comment on the fact that the troops had nothing to do, now that the enemy was retreating and almost the whole province was under rebel command. 'We've become fat boas,' he dictated, 'and if this continues I'm coming over there to work with you, since there's more danger on Broadway than there is here.' The aide-de-camp, who was taking down the letter, asked how to spell Broadway.

THE BLACK GENERAL NEVER GOT TO SEE PARIS. In a brief clash, which seemed more like a skirmish, he was shot dead. He had just turned around to his aide-de-camp to tell him, 'This is going well!' when a bullet knocked him off his horse.

The enemy noticed the confusion that arose among the *mambí* troops, without knowing why, and thickened its fire upon the alarmed rebels, killing or wounding several who attempted to recover the corpse.

As the rebels retreated, the enemy raked the area until they found the body of the black general. They searched and emptied his pockets, as they always did, without realizing whom they had killed.

It was not until sunset that a rebel patrol could come and retrieve the half-naked corpse. Beside the general lay his aide-de-camp, who, incidentally, was the son of the commander-in-chief.

A REBEL SHOUTS: 'They killed the general!' and the troops are demoralized. A lieutenant kills the rebel with a shot in the back and stands up. 'The general is not dead!' he shouts left and right. 'The commander-in-chief is alive!' The rebels reassemble their forces and advance upon the enemy, winning the battle when it seemed lost.

BEFORE LAUNCHING THE INVASION, the Americans sent a message to the general with the star on his forehead, who had promised to give them support.

The day before the landing, the general with the star on his forehead met with two American generals, to agree on their strategy against their common enemy.

The Cuban troops were transported in American warships to take part in the first and only battle the invaders fought. 'On the day of the landing,' says an enemy historian, 'it [the city] was deprived of all the resources it normally received from its farm regions, and a famine resulted; communications were cut off; forests, avenues and hills were all covered with Cubans.'

Finally, after a short and almost ridiculous naval battle, the city surrendered to the enemy, which in this case were the friends.

THE OLD COMMANDER-IN-CHIEF was nicknamed the Chinaman because he was inscrutable. He entered the capital with a disjointed hand in a sling. As a future president would say before a similar disability, it was all 'a casualty in the war of hands'. So many times had his right hand been shaken from one end of the island to the other that he came to be wary of a hand being wielded in front of him. It was for him a new enemy weapon in friendly hands.

His entry into the capital was a moment of glory with crowds surrounding him literally everywhere. The old commander-in-chief couldn't get over his amazement, so he remarked: 'Good God, if we had as many troops as admirers, we would have felled the whole Spanish army with a feather!' And he added, shaking his head like an old Chinaman, 'With one single feather!'

IT'S A RADIANT DAY. The sun is shining intensely up above and the transparent air flutters the flag. The flag will be flying for the first time. Ambassadors and plenipotentiary ministers have gathered on the platform. The newly inaugurated president is also there. Generals and colonels have congregated around the flagpole as well. They have just lowered the Stars and Stripes and the flag with the solitary star is flying out in the open. The day is not only radiant but also auspicious – but this cannot be seen in the photograph.

AFTER INDEPENDENCE, the general with the legendary name (known for his manner of capturing, interrogating and exterminating Spanish *guerrilleros* by saying: 'What's your name?' and then, after the prisoner's answer, adding an ominous ' . . . 'twas his name') rebelled against the government in a little war that lasted a few days. But it cost him his life. They found him at dawn, still asleep, and with a machete sliced his head off and sent it to the capital. Years after, they erected a grotesque statue of him in a square in the capital. This time he had his head on his shoulders.

THERE WAS A REVOLT OF BLACK SOLDIERS, led by a black politician and a veteran of the war of independence who was also black. It was a minor revolt, but not so minor as to be excluded from the history books. People still speak of it under their breath. The truth is that the leaders were caught and shot immediately. In the brief war more than three thousand persons had died, all of them, as one historian says, 'coloured people'.

THE HAITIAN AND JAMAICAN WORKERS sent a delegation to speak with the plantation owner. They had decided to end the strike if they received the salary increase. All seemed to be going perfectly well and the owner suggested that they take a picture of the group to commemorate the agreement. The Haitian and Jamaican delegates stood in a row in front of the machine, which was covered by a black cloth. The owner left the group to give an order to his foreman. The foreman uncovered the machine and calmly machine-gunned the group of delegates. There were no more complaints from the sugar-cane workers during that harvest and for many to come.

The story could be true or false. But the times made it believable.

THE GENERAL ASKED WHAT TIME IT WAS and an aide-de-camp quickly ran to his side and mumbled: 'Any time you wish, Mr President.'

THE FIRST CAR came as far as the little iron bridge, made a U-turn and then stopped, forcing the second car – larger and lower – to stop too. A third car sprang out from the trees and then stopped. Guns emerged from each window. A sawn-off shotgun fired at the big car, spraying it from left to right. While the black chauffeur of the big car threw himself on the floor, the passenger in the back seat fell as only the dead fall. It was then that the first car completed its U-turn and, also firing upon the big car, this time from right to left, made off in the opposite direction. The two attacking cars drove away together at a leisurely pace.

THEY DUG A TUNNEL under the street from the little house to the cemetery. They continued digging to the private mausoleum – it was more of a mausoleum than a tomb – making their way through bones and rotting coffins. They dug incessantly to reach the private mausoleum before the funeral. They continued digging through the mud and the carrion flesh and they say that one of the diggers lost his mind. They continued digging until after the assassination, and the same day that the illustrious dead man's funeral was to take place they buried the dynamite and rammed the wires through the tunnel and to the house. They were ready by the time of the burial, but the burial didn't take place. Everything – the assassination, the tunnel, the dynamite – turned out to be a waste because the illustrious dead man's family decided to bury him in his home town and not in the family mausoleum in Havana. They were able to recover the dynamite, but it was impossible to refill the tunnel and they decided to forget about the wires, which were discovered by a grave-digger a few days later, while he was digging.

THE BLACK MAN PORTRAYED IN THE PHOTO is a Cuban dandy. The photograph was taken by a famous American photographer in Old Havana *circa* 1932 and the dandy in white could be a *sbirro*. He is dressed to kill anyway. He wears a three-piece white linen suit with a spotless white shirt, a black necktie tied in a narrow knot and display handkerchief. There are two white Cubans dressed in shabby dark suits standing next to him and he seems to be listening to their conversation in a casual manner. Both men are middle-aged and wear horn-rimmed glasses but the black man has piercing black eyes. Obviously he doesn't need glasses. The black in white does not seem to be with the white men after all. As a matter of fact he doesn't seem to be with anybody. He is standing alone and aloof next to a popular *bodega* bar. The three men have one thing in common though: they all wear white straw hats. Boaters were all the rage in Cuba at the time. But the straw hat looks better on the black man. Hats always do.

The black man in white could very well be a *porrista*, one of those toughies who were with the dictator's political police, *la Porra*. But if he is a *porrista* he is at least an elegant one. To complete his attire he is wearing very shiny black shoes, so shiny and so black that they look like patent-leather loafers. Actually his shoes had been recently shined by the bootblack we can see in the near background. He is a nondescript mulatto who appears to be kneeling before his throne-like shoeshine chair, now empty. The shoeshine man has a peg leg, seen protruding from his left trouser leg: the wooden leg shines like a shoe. Behind the bootblack a blond boy is seated on the steps of the enormous chair. He is a newsboy and he is obviously having a monologue with the one-legged shoeshine who is reading a newspaper.

In the background but somewhat central there is also a news-stand. There are many magazines and newspapers hanging from the racks, firmly held with clothes pins. The magazines are American and Cuban but all the newspapers are local. The bestselling newspaper was the Government's mouthpiece but when the dictator fled its building was burnt down by a political mob. There are many copies of a magazine that was the most popular weekly then. In its present issue, if you could buy a copy, you would find an article, almost an editorial, which stated that the dictator was a great Cuban and a great man who was all for peace among Cubans. A few issues later the same editorial will condemn the fallen dictator as a tyrant now in exile, but it will extol the civic virtues of the new strong man, a great Cuban no doubt.

None of this has happened yet. Right now everything is fixed in time by the photograph and the moment seems eternal. The dangerous dandy will keep his eyes skinned as he watches the invisible photographer, black on white, for ever.

THEY HID IN A HOUSE on Esperanza Street. It seemed like one of those ironies of fate, as they say, but that's how it was. They said to the man who came to the door: 'Please, sir, hide us. We are being chased by Tyranny.' This is also true: that's what they said. How they turned that terrible, but then personal, moment into a generalization, almost into an abstract thought, how they did it, nobody knows, but it is known that they did it. They hid in a house on Esperanza Street and the police came and took them out on the street and killed them near the market. But that was later. Now what really matters, what is really moving, is to know that those three boys, persecuted, half naked (one of them barefoot), said: 'We're being chased by Tyranny,' and not: 'We're being chased by the police,' or 'by the army'. No, they said precisely that they were being chased by Tyranny and that's what made them heroes.

Shouldn't one believe that if there is a poetic intuition, there is also a historical intuition?

TWO OTHERS HID on the outskirts of the town. It was very early, but some neighbour saw them or they asked if they could go into another house first. What's certain is that they began searching the houses and someone told them that there were people hiding there (pointing). They looked and didn't find anything. And they were going when someone on the street told them that they did see people go in, that they didn't know whether or not they were the ones from the assault, but that they saw them. They went back to the house and found one coming out of a water tank in the patio. He had been inside it all the time. Two soldiers made him get back in. They kept him under the water at gunpoint and each time he came out they made him go down again. If the head came up out of an instinct of preservation or a reflex or the laws of hydraulics, they pushed it down with their rifle butts. Until he drowned. Then they took him out and threw him on to the patio as if they had just caught an unwanted fish.

The other was hidden in the hollow of the A-frame roof, but they saw him now. They began telling him to come down; he started running along the tiles, he ran along the rain gutter, bending down as he crossed the ridge of the roof. He didn't hear or didn't want to hear the orders to stop. He ran faster, perhaps pushed by the decline of the upper slope. He reached the eaves, stopped, put one foot on the drainpipe. He felt it give way. He saw that on the other side was only the corner of the building and the street. He ran – again in the direction of the patio. He was running slowly, with difficulty, up the roof when one of the soldiers said: Leave it, Sergeant, don't shout any more – I'll get him down. When the sergeant looked sternly at the soldier, saying: I don't want anybody to go up, the soldier said: I said that I'd get him down, not that I'd go up. The sergeant remained silent, and the boy was still running up the roof when the soldier took aim and fired.

SHE WAS DOING THE WASH ON THE PATIO when they brought her the news. She didn't say anything or cry or show any emotion. She simply asked: Is it true? The man, the one who spoke, because there were three of them, said yes with his head and explained. They mentioned his name on the radio along with two other compañeros. He had his hat in his hand and now he slapped his leg with it. We know that the official report was false, he said. All that about a battle and killed in action is a shameless lie, of course. It was from another source that we learned how it happened. They arrested them and took them to headquarters and killed them there, he said. Then they concocted the skirmish. She looked at them and didn't say anything. She was forty, maybe younger, but she looked like an old woman. She wore a tattered dress with little purple flowers and her hair gathered in a bun. Her eyes were a very pale yellow-green and it seemed as if the midday light bothered her. In the silence now she could hear the wind between the trees in the patio and a hen cackling. You'll excuse me, she said, but I have to go on with the wash.

She finished and went into the house and made coffee. She drank it standing, in the doorway, watching how the air became visible between the sheets.

THE CROWD CAME OUT TO CELEBRATE the fall of the dictator. But it was a false alarm. The demonstrators who marched toward the presidential palace were stopped by a machine gun stationed at the palace entrance. Many managed to hide in the fountain in the middle of the park. Others ran to hide behind the trees. And others did an about-face and tried to run away. These suffered the most casualties, mowed down by the machine-gun fire. There are those who say that the false news of his flight had been circulated by the tyrant himself, a few days before he really had to abdicate.

THE PHOTOGRAPH IS CURIOUSLY SYMBOLIC. It signals the end of a military tyranny at the same time it glorifies a soldier. All the points of the picture converge towards the soldier, who is standing on top of the statue of a lion at the beginning of an avenue in the capital. The soldier is erect, his rifle raised in his right hand, while his left stretches toward one side, perhaps to aid his balance. His head is held high and proud, celebrating the moment of triumph, which is, apparently, collective.

At the extreme left-hand side of the picture, one of the demonstrators has taken off his boater and salutes upwards, towards the soldier. To the right and in the centre, another, more modest demonstrator (in shirt-sleeves) takes off his cap while he cheers the soldier. They are all surrounded by a small mob, excited by the triumph of its cause, it seems.

Behind the soldier you can see some wrought-iron balconies and some windows with their French shutters wide open. Further away, in the corner, there's an advertisement for an airline company, in English. The photograph has been reproduced all over as a testimony to its era – or rather of its moment.

ONE OF THE TWO BOYS who pushed open the swinging
doors of the bar was barely sixteen. The other was so thin
and fragile that in his hands the Colt .45 seemed like a
submachine gun. Both walked up to the counter. 'Move
aside, gentlemen,' the older boy said. 'Our business is
with this one,' he said, pointing to a police lieutenant
who was calmly drinking at one end of the counter. The
customers moved away and the lieutenant barely had time
to place the glass on the counter when the bullets reached
him. He fell to the floor, dead, and they gave him a *coup
de grâce* in the temple. Then both walked out of the bar,
quietly, with stealth. Unfortunately for the young killers,
the lieutenant belonged to a rival gang. Since they had
acted on their own and the leader of their group was
fearful of reprisals, instead of taking them in and hiding
them, he handed them over to the leader of the rival gang.
The next morning the boy who was barely sixteen and the
skinny, fragile boy were found shot to death beside the
little lake at the Country Club.

WHEN THEY RAN OUT OF AMMUNITION they decided to surrender. There was a corpse in the garden, beside the jacaranda. They couldn't recognize the person when they passed because he had fallen face down. He was wearing a yellow pullover and the man who came down from the porch on to the path wondered who had been wearing a yellow pullover that day. He could glimpse, beyond the gate and on the pavement, another dead civilian. But he didn't try to guess who it could be, because he no longer thought about the dead, only about the soldiers and police beyond the garden gate. Like the others, he was unarmed: that's the condition they demanded over the loudspeakers. 'You are surrounded! Throw your weapons and come out with your hands on your head', they said over and over. He decided to surrender. Now he saw, out on the pavement, the first man to surrender, carrying the wounded child. He saw him being arrested and the police swarming around him. He and the pregnant woman passed under the sign that said Villa Carmita and as he thought she was tripping, slipping and falling, he tried to help her. He never could. The two fell together as the volley knocked them down like nine-pins. On the ground he was still trying to lift the woman who was already dead when on his *guayabera* shirt several red stains burst out. Pushed by the impact he slid back, recoiled against the wall and landed on the garden path. He was dead of course but the bullets went on hitting him. One of the columns of the gate was splintered and the sand and brick splattered about.

IT WAS A STRATEGY invented in Chicago during the late twenties but perfected here. One car comes first and sprays the marked house with bullets. The occupants or residents come out on the street, frightened and angered, and begin to shoot at the speeding car. Precisely at that moment another car comes by at top speed and shoots at them, wounding and killing a good many. Now the ploy was being used in a very unorthodox manner. The one who was marked to die was chatting at the entrance of a movie theatre, some say with a friend, while others say the friend was a decoy. In any case, the fact is that one car sped by, spraying the entrance of the theatre, shooting haphazardly, without aiming. The man who was to die managed to hide behind a parked car. When the shooting was over he came out of his hiding place, and before he reached the lobby the bullets got him: this time they were fired by two men on foot. The two gunmen quickly but calmly walked away. The friend (or decoy) had remained hidden under a car. The one who was to die died, as one writer described it, with only thirty-five cents in his pocket.

IT WAS 9 P.M. and the senator was having toast and coffee in his favourite café. At that moment two men came in, took out their pistols and shot the senator. Innocent or guilty, the senator was eating bread when they killed him, and his white linen suit was stained with blood and spilled coffee.

IT BEGAN TO RAIN when the parade passed in front of the national Capitol. An aide-de-camp came running with an umbrella. He opened it. 'Mr President, don't get wet.' The president of the republic made a gracious gesture with his hand, and, refusing the umbrella, answered: 'It's of no importance, *amigo*. This is Cuban water that's falling.'

THE GENERAL HAD BEEN TWICE A PRESIDENT and he is now a civilian, though his more consuming passion is to be a president again. Does he have a philosophy of life? Perhaps a political thought? Or even a belief in democracy? None whatsoever. But he loved power more than he ever loved any woman. Power was the spur. He craved after power, he suffered from lust for power. He would have sold his soul to the devil (which he is about to do) for one more moment of power. To get it he even consented to being a candidate, just one more candidate, in the next elections. It is now March and he had learnt the meaning of the Ides of March. Punning in Spanish he said he couldn't let the *Idus* become *idos:* gone for ever. He had just received two complementary bits of news, like sine and cosine of his future. First the bad news: he came last in the polls which asked only one question: who do you think should be our next president? He would never be an elected president again. The good news now: some officers in the army were ready to stage a coup and they all wanted him to be the leader as before. His first reaction was to say no: they all were too young to succeed. Then he remembered that he was even younger at the time of his first coup. He asked them for time to consider their offer. Under his pillow he always kept a Walther pistol just in case. Inadvertently, as he tossed about in bed, he found his pistol. He caressed it: an iron weapon for an iron will. Next morning he said to them you're on or words to that effect. They were all ready for a coup that would be the most momentous act of his life and a wicked action against the people. He was ready. He took the Walther pistol with him.

It was, as he was wont to say, a decision before dawn,

without realizing how trite the phrase was. He was not popular but he was a vulgar man. After the coup mechanism, which he knew well, was in motion there was no turning back, hence the pistol. He had to enter alone and unarmed the military camp which was the biggest in all Central America. After identifying himself to the guard at Gate 5 he should go to general headquarters, which he also knew well as he had built it. There he would meet all the officers who would be his general staff. At the last moment, however, sensing foul play, he kept his Walther at hand and he chose Gate 6 to gain entrance to the camp. The guard at Gate 6 was not waiting for him. In fact he didn't even know him and was very wary. The general, about to become once more the General or a dead body, ordered the hesitant guard to stand to attention. The sentry really didn't know what to do: to let this crazy man in, to arrest him or just to kill him. The intruder felt his pistol in his jacket side-pocket. He was considering killing the sentry on the spot but he feared the noise and the commotion and what is worse, to commit an act of violence when he should be presented as the harbinger of peace.

The two men became immobile facing each other in the early morning. Then, as several times before in his life, the general invoked the old Cuban Indian spirits: he was calling at the gate of all dead Indians that were immortal. Then he intoned an orison for peace among all Cubans. He thought he had prayed for ever though he only did it for a few seconds. Suddenly there was a bright light only he, The Man, could see: a light that didn't come from the sunrise that should be late in March. Or from the camp at a distance or from a car's headlights or from a lamppost in the street. It was a light marvellous – it was a gloriole, but he didn't know the word for he was an ignoramus. It was a halo, a nimbus, an aura. But he knew what it was: it was the Light of Yara. Yara, a mere village now, had been for centuries the religious centre for all Cuban Indians, dead or alive. He considered himself a descendant of the Arawaks of lore and he was particularly pleased when he was called *el Indio* or Indian Chief. Now the Light of Yara once more came to bathe him in glory: the general was about to become the General again. The Light of Yara was flooding him: he had become an Immortal. The sentry let him go into history. Though at the time he called it eternity.

That was, literally, his version of the *coup d'état* that became, actually, a *coup de grâce*. He had, in fact, killed the republic – without firing a shot.

THE AMBITIOUS GENERAL appears, surrounded by army officers, but he's dressed in civilian clothes. This is his third *coup d'état* in twenty years and he looks smugly satisfied with his prowess. The general, who likes symbols, is wearing a leather jacket: the same one he wore previously on similar occasions. Later he will swear that in his jacket pocket he always carried a pistol with 'one bullet in the chamber' – to kill or to die if his *coup d'état* failed. But he risked very little, with the commander of the army caught sleeping in his long johns. The general is in the middle of the photograph, with a caption that says: 'He is The Man!' That *ecce homo* is meant to be flattering. The general, in civilian clothes, is smiling, perhaps thinking of the historical forces he has just unleashed, but it doesn't show. Around him are colonels and captains who will soon be, in barely a few hours, generals and brigadiers. This strong-armed promotion will divide the island in two. But it doesn't seem to matter to the men in the picture.

THE MAN, a tall mulatto with long, thin hands and legs so long that when he stood up it was as if he were on stilts: he seemed to unfold, to unroll like an accordion of bones and put himself together in midair, join the infinite parts compactly, stick out his thin, narrow and also long chest, and finally gain his balance. Now he had on a white or yellow pale straw skimmer which he wore with the brim up, like the urban blacks, who don't believe in the sun. His face was bony and thin and also impregnable, not because of the dark glasses he wore, but because of itself, hermetic except when he laughed and showed one or two gold teeth. His laughter was his true communication, his laughter and the guitar which between his large hands, poised on his prayerless mantis arms, looked like a violin, a mandolin, a bandore: it was crossed over his chest, yellow against the white undershirt revealed under the black-and-white-striped shirt, clean, neatly buttoned, decorated with the great gold medallion of the Virgen de la Caridad del Cobre, the shirt opened to reveal the immaculate interior (like white teeth over the chest and the doubly golden image). He laughed while he played God knows what Longina or Santa Cecilia or 'On the Path of my Sad Life' or something like that and he let the notes linger, reach the half tone, stop as if on an endless melisma, in a warble, and stretch beyond the palm trees and the *copetúas* in bloom, well over the leafy fire of the flame tree, reproduced in the sunset: in the cosmic fire which exploded, drew back, and again burst beyond the purple, blue, black hills – in an incredible, unique free solar show which interested no one now.

Life, friend, is like that dead cow, he said when he finished playing and crossed his hands over the guitar,

72

covering it. See the dead cow? Nobody can make you go back, he said to the boy, nor can the jeep go in reverse nor the post-office clock slow down, 'cause none of that ain't goin' to save the cow. So the best thing is for each to go his own way: the cow to the slaughter so's the butcher can complete what you guys began, he said, looking toward the boy, who was a recruit, but also toward the corporal and the other soldier in the jeep, who got out at the young driver's insistence to make excuses for the run-over cow. Where were you guys going in such a hurry, you people here go home and go on doing what you were doing, he said, looking toward the regretful farmer behind him, back home to your dead season's misery, and me, I'm going to keep playing until the invisible machine one day, without a sound, catches up with me and my guitar . . . One of those songs or speeches of yours ought to get stuck in your throat like a sweet potato without lard and choke you, you hear me, said the corporal, staring at him. You never know, Corporal, the black man said. You never know. It's like I say: in life, anything can happen. The corporal noisily planted his boot on the wooden floor of the town's grocery-post-office-mayor's office-bar-social club-veterans' centre and he shook one hand, pointing a twisted forefinger at the musician. Listen to what I'm telling you, he said, you damn nigger. Black man, the black man said. No, not black man, damn nigger, said the threatening corporal. Just like you say, Corporal; you're the law and God's Gospel and the corporal, said the black man without moving a finger from the guitar, without moving backwards or forwards, without taking his eyes off the corporal or the three soldiers. Well, said the corporal, you're a damn nigger and a big-mouth and we've got a file on you. So you take your music elsewhere. I don't want to see you around here when we come back. Take my advice.

73

Remember the cow. I won't forget the cow, Corporal, the black man said. Thanks for the advice. Take his word for it, boy, said the other soldier. Remember the cow, repeated the corporal, moving his finger. Let's go, Corporal, said the boy, the driver, the recruit, please, because if not we'll still be on the road when night comes. What? You afraid? No, Corporal, not afraid, but we don't have lights: the cow made a mess of our headlights. The cow? Not the cow – you knocked into her. I followed your orders, Corporal, said the boy. Yes, I told you to run but not to crash, said the corporal with finality and then he turned back to the black man: Remember, I don't want to see you or your guitar or your songs, not even a peep, when I come back, you hear me. The black man said: Just like you say, Corporal.

They left. Before the jeep even started, after being inspected again, and the sun was already hiding, in the indifference of those on the porch looking only at the soldiers, the black man slipped a casual hand over the strings, which sounded what seemed like a chord but was actually the final point of the incident. And when they really left, when they went past the protective curve and beyond the last house of town, the black man played again and sang again and again laughed as he had played, sung and laughed before the soldiers came, when they killed the cow, when they got out of the jeep still stunned by the blow or the surprise, when they came into the house, when they looked for the owner and found his music and his laughter and his lazy way, which would stay there, without the slightest doubt, after the last soldier, after the last dead animal (or man) and after the last jeep that was hurried or fearful or both came by.

He was singing 'Pretty Maria' with the music of Agustín Lara and the corporal's lyrics:

Remember the cow,
Pretty Maria, my Maria,
Remember her eyes, dear,
So sleepy and so brown. . .

THE NIGHT BEFORE, around 2 a.m., the one who seemed to be the leader came in to tell them that they were going to attack the garrison. He didn't tell them which garrison. He said that those who weren't in favour could refuse to join. He would only ask them to stay at the farm for at least two hours after the others left. It would be a security measure for those who weren't going as much as for those who were. One of the men spoke. He was not in favour of the attack. He didn't even know why he was there. He had come with some friends to the carnival. He thought the attack would fail. Nevertheless, he added, I'll go. Two others decided not to go. It's curious. The man who went on the attack without being in favour of it fought, behaved perfectly, and was wounded, but his life was spared. Of the seven who remained in the house, not one survived. The police, the army, the secret service, or whatever, discovered the place, surrounded the dwelling and made them come out, shouting at them with a loudspeaker to surrender. They killed them as they came out, one by one.

THERE'S A POPULAR SAYING that when a black man has grey hairs it's because he's old and free of cares. This black man, this man, was old, but walked nimbly and fearlessly down the street although not far off you could still hear occasional shots and from time to time a burst of machine-gun fire, clear, distinctly among the usual sounds of dawn: crowing roosters, birds twittering in the trees, a window opening and a gate banging against an iron railing. He went up Caridad Street with the bread under his arm and greeted someone who passed by. He turned on Espinosa and upon reaching Sebastián Castro and Saldaña streets he heard the engine. He saw the jeep's headlights, still on, appear, and then the whole vehicle, coming over the top of the hill, and he also saw the soldiers. The jeep passed alongside him; he kept on going. Then he heard someone, from behind, calling his name. He turned around and received the shots in his chest, neck and head.

Of course they knew him; everybody in the city knew him: he was a revolutionary years ago and had been in prison and escaped death many times. But not this time. He had been sick a week and since he lived alone, had to go out to buy his breakfast. Everybody knew him and he was lying on the street, dead, with the bread over the pool of blood, until noon or later. He was left lying there as an example, or rather a symbol, of the times when it was his turn to die – which were, like those of all men, bad times to live in.

THE ONLY THING ALIVE IS THE HAND. In any case, the hand seems alive leaning on the wall. One can't see the arm and perhaps the hand is dead too. Perhaps it's the hand of an eyewitness and the spot on the wall is its shadow and other shadows as well. Below, half a yard below, the lawn is burnt by the July sun. There are burnt spots in the grass, from footsteps or dirt or cement paths. Now the paths seem bleached, shiny, from the sunlight. A nearby object – a grenade, the shell of a high-calibre cannon, a movie camera? – looks black, like a hole in the photograph. On the path, all over the lawn, there are four – no, five – plain pinewood boxes. (There seem to be six, but that last coffin is the shadow of the wall.) One of the boxes is half opened and there's a corpse in it, beside the nearest box there's another corpse, its arm hanging out, as if beckoning. The box one can see better, on the right, is nailed and ready for its journey. In the middle of the courtyard there's a solitary corpse, who doesn't have a coffin either but awaits one, bent awkwardly, with a garbage can over his head, placed there out of compassion or perhaps mockery. Some trees in the background project a dark shadow. Above, to the left, a wrought-iron hook blends in with the dark trees and looks like a sign. It is only a decoration on the wall or the balcony of the barracks.

ALL THAT'S LEFT OF HIM is a photograph and the memory.

In the photograph he's sitting on the floor and looks at the photographer as he will look at death, serenely. He is wounded; you can see blood flowing down his right leg and a dark stain (the wound) on his thigh – and it's not a *cornada*. So nobody is running to carry the bullfighter to the infirmary. This is not a bullfight and the floor of Moorish glazed tiles is not that of a chapel in a small-town bullring. It's army headquarters, during carnival, on a Sunday. The wounded man did not put on a *traje de luces*, because he's not a *novillero*, nor did he wish to pose as a matador. He tried to put an end to tyranny and dressed up as a soldier at dawn and came to attack the barracks with ninety other boys. Now the attack has failed and he is lying there on the floor of the guard post waiting to be interrogated. He's not afraid nor does he feel pain, but he's not bragging or even thinking of pain or fear: he is coming to his end with the same simplicity with which he behaved at the beginning – and he waits.

Memory knows that seconds later they made him stand up, pushed him around, knocked the cigarette out of his mouth and cursed at him. The photographer gave him the cigarette, the very same man who naïvely thought he could save him with the photograph. They shouted questions at him and he calmly answered that he didn't know anything and couldn't say anything: You are the authorities, not me. They say that only once did he try to touch his wound with his hand, but couldn't, and even though he made no grimace you could see that it hurt like hell. Later they shoved him out, beating him with their gun butts, and when he was limping down the three steps that

79

led to the courtyard they shot him in the back of the head.
His hands were still tied, as they are in the photograph.

THEY MADE THEM LINE UP in the prison courtyard. There were five or six, all political prisoners. It was 24 December, and an interrogation at night, out in the cold open air, is no Christmas Eve. It was all dark around the prison and you could hear the wind whipping over the roof. Two searchlights were focused on them. Soldiers and not the usual guards were the watchmen. The interrogator, dressed in a colonel's uniform, asked something, first in a low voice, and then he shouted curses at them for several minutes, exhausting his vocabulary of foul words, repeating them, and beginning again, he would again talk quietly, as if chatting.

Then a lieutenant, who always remained in the dark, put a pistol behind their ears one by one. The colonel shouted each time: Are you going to talk, sonofabitch, are you going to talk? and between the end of his shout and the shot you could hear the silence or the wind.

They had been prisoners for days and none could answer the questions about an armed attack made that morning. Before dying, did the last hostage think he was dreaming?

LIKE MANY CUBANS, he enjoyed making jokes about sexual perversions, and his speciality was the perfect imitation of a faggot. A thin, small mulatto, he'd comb his hair with a hot comb and make an impeccable duck-tail. At first when he joined the group, they gave him a certain nickname; but then he revealed that he was brave and cool-headed and daring enough to choose his own alias. He should have been a dancer in peacetime because he did the rumba really well, but now he was a terrorist and soon he became the provincial organizer of terrorist action and sabotage, which was a job not everybody could aspire to. Political terrorism is not what you might call child's play. And if it's play, it must be similar to Russian roulette.

One of this terrorist's favourite devices was to fasten a stick of dynamite securely at his waist, light the wick under his jacket, and then let the stick roll down inside his pants, while he calmly strolled along. A little after he had perfected this trick, he was caught.

Walking up the steps of the precinct, handcuffed to a policeman, he was wondering how he would escape torture, when he thought up a trick. It might work. He was dressed, as always, in jeans with his shirt hanging out and white sneakers, and he walked up the last steps gaily, with almost winged feet, wiggling his hips. As he went in, he smoothed his hair with his free hand, shaping his curl at the same time. The policemen looked at him in surprise. When the sergeant on duty asked him his name and address, he gave in a singsong voice a false name and a false address and an occupation that was also false: window dresser. Those who arrested him insisted that he be marked down as dangerous and the sergeant looked him up and down again. This meant that he had to be seen by the chief of the precinct. The policemen vouched that he was the head of a terrorist organization and at their insistence the chief came out. Upon hearing the door open and the military steps and seeing the respectful attention with which everybody saluted, he turned around with a gesture that he had thought graceful, and swinging only his hips, he confronted his nemesis and the bodyguards with an almost erotic smile. It was a captain who had begun his career at the same time as the terrorist, but in another direction. The two men looked at each other and the terrorist humbly lowered his long eyelashes. The captain burst out in a hearty laugh and shouted amid the general laughter: Goddamn it, how many times do I have to tell you to leave the fags alone! Nobody protested: who would dare? They let the terrorist go and he went out thanking them in a florid, languid lisp.

But the story has another less graceful ending. Two or three months later they caught him again, this time with a carful of weapons. The captain wanted to interrogate him personally and when he greeted him he reminded the terrorist of their previous interview. He was found a week later in the gutter. They had cut off his tongue and stuck it in his anus.

THE SIERRA IS NOT A LANDSCAPE; it's a scenic backdrop. Before you reach it there is the red and yellow savannah, with torrential rivers or dry riverbeds or endless grass, or yellow burnt hay or great clouds of dust, depending on the season and weather. And there are the sugar mills, the farm, the cattle ranches: sugar cane and fruit trees and cattle by the thousands. On the other side (one hundred and fifty miles away) is the sea, in waves which sculpt the rocks into abstract coral statues or pebbles or narrow beaches, and (sometimes just with the tide) the mountains plunge down into the ocean. Or there are the mangroves, the swamp: inlets of mire and mosquitoes. On the base of the mountains there's tropical vegetation and maybe coconut and palm trees. There is also the underbush growing at night over the path cleared that morning. Sometimes there are bread trees and *curujey* parasite plants among the branches of the *ceiba* and the *dagame* trees, to aid the traveller dying of thirst or hunger, and as pretty decorations he will have the wild orchids. Perhaps he'll find purple star apples or a stray mango or wild papayas and surely sweet custard apples and guavas and trees of rare wood, if the nomadic charcoal merchant didn't get there first. Further up there are no more fruit trees and he begins to find giant ferns and the cork palm and other plants that were there before the deluge. But the jungle is still with him: it's a world of vegetation, though it's possible that he'll see Cuban boas, which are harmless to man. He will also see the *hutia*, that enormous edible rat, and many, many birds. He'll probably find the strange spectacle of a dead tree blossoming turkey buzzards. Or perhaps another tree with a nest of *caracaras* on the point of falling because of the weight. He'll see hummingbirds

84

that look like insects, and butterflies the size of birds. His path will now be blocked by the *tibisí* plant, which replaces the *marabú* and the thorn bushes as vegetal dikes: the machete barely scratches it. Here and there he will see a tubular tree trunk a yard or two in diameter; it's the barrel tree, which on the bottom is like a savannah bush and on the top is a perfect living casket.

The air becomes thin and sometimes the traveller is surrounded by clouds and when they're like a rug it's because there's a precipice below. You walk between abysses along passages a half-metre wide, and one thousand five hundred, one thousand eight hundred, two thousand metres high. The slopes are vertical and the only points of support for foot or hand in precarious hold are roots and bushes and some hard stone. When you reach a plateau, everything is green: even the sunlight is green. The ground is covered with a herbaceous green carpet; the trees, bushes and jungle run the whole gamut of green. Tree trunks are covered with a lichen that is like green rust and wet to the touch: that green reality is moist. Thousands of pearls of rain drip from the leaves, and as you step, the grass sinks with a crackling watery sound. On the mossy rocks you find liquid-like glass and your path is crossed with tiny streams, veins of water. The temperature is a few degrees above freezing and light barely penetrates the foliage. In a clearing there's a rag of a cloud and the sun tears it and along the rays climbs a spiral stream of vapour. There's no breeze, but once in a while we all feel a cold gust of wind. Far below is the grey sea on one side, and on the other the savannah now looks grey.

THE DAY THEY CAME THE WAR WAS GOING BADLY. They appeared without warning, like paratroopers. The sentry rejected them, telling them they couldn't stay and that they should go back where they'd come from. They didn't want to, and an officer had to be brought over and they didn't go then either. The camp wasn't very large and the noise reached the head comandante's quarters and the comandante came out. He saw the group, came over to discover what was happening and found the soldiers in an argument with an average-looking farmer and a guy who was so small that he made the other look like a giant. What's going on here? the comandante asked. These guys, who came without weapons and don't want to go back, answered the guard. Is that right? the comandante asked. Yes, said the little guy, and when he stood next to the comandante, who's six foot two, he became a dwarf. The commander looked him up and down, but the other in turn looked him up and down, and they didn't say anything. The comandante smoked his perpetual cigar, moved it from one side of his mouth to the other and exhaled thick smoke, which the small visitor perceived as clouds. They looked like St George and the Dragon of the lithographs and they soon would be David and Goliath. No weapons, eh, said the comandante without asking. You can't stay here without weapons, he said, raising his voice. Go back where you came from. We don't have weapons, or food either, he said, and we're not going to be feeding idle mouths. The midget looked at him once more; he seemed to stand on tiptoe, prepare his sling and throw the stone: So if you didn't have weapons, how come you called the people to come fight?

Now the comandante was the one who was disarmed

and he could only answer: OK, Captain, let them stay. But if in the first skirmish, he said, they don't even get only one shotgun, shoot them for me, 'cause we already have enough dead weight, what with our impedimenta, to be carrying around live weights as well. The two newcomers stayed, although they never knew if the comandante had been joking or not. In the next battle the bigger guy didn't pick up any enemy weapon and didn't return to camp. The midget, however, captured a Springfield which was larger than he. Then he fought so much and so well that he soon became a captain and when he died, three days before the war was over, they made him a comandante posthumously.

HE PRETENDED TO MEET HIM BY CHANCE and greet him as you greet an old friend you haven't seen for some time. The other was having beer and he also ordered beer. When the waiter brought the two beers and left, the man who had just got there said to the other man, in a whisper: 'The bird's in the cage.' The first one, who had already been at the café – that thirty-year-old man who looks forty because of his premature bald spot and the black shadow of his beard and the heavy moustache, but also because of the bitter expression in his eyes, at the corners of his lips, in his mouth when he speaks, a grimace like the wake of an old suffering – almost smiling, says, 'So he finally came. Great, that's great.' He was truly smiling now. 'It's curtains for him today,' he said.

They asked for another beer and silently toasted success, in what was not precisely a business deal. It was past eleven in the morning and they were still sitting out al fresco, watching the clear end of the winter day curve upward into a cloudless sky over the calm blue sea, and their eyes followed the cars rushing by along the avenue. A tall blonde girl crossed the street, beautiful and perhaps a bit fat, but Rubens wouldn't think so – nor did the first man, who looked her up and down and threw her a compliment as she passed. After a while another woman crossed: a thin, almond-eyed mulatto, moving her hips as she walked. He threw her a compliment too. The other man, who was shy, smiled at his companion's exclamations of flattery and sipped a little beer. Many women passed the sidewalk café and he always offered each words of praise, talking in his funny Spanish accent. The other seemed to watch him in amusement, but deep down in admiration of a man who in two or three hours would

88

lead an attack on the presidential palace, the most difficult of the commando operations, and would perhaps be dead (and he would), who now seemed a superficial, frivolous and peaceful citizen: a content accountant having his midday aperitif.

IF A FEW ADVERSE CIRCUMSTANCES can be called Destiny, then the surprise attack on the presidential palace in Havana was destined to fail. As it was written that the ambitious army stenographer who rose from being just a sergeant to the rank of colonel in twenty-four hours and even had the effrontery to pin the stars of a general on himself, he who years later became the dictator the would-be assassins came to kill in his official residence, this hated man would die in bed of natural causes in a golden exile in Europe decades later: this too was written.

The vehicles that were carrying the guerrilla force got bogged down in the afternoon traffic in a city they all knew by heart. Why didn't they take into account the perennial jams after lunch? Nobody knows. Be that as it may two of the cars reached the back door of the palace on time. The front gate of the building opened only on memorable occasions: ambassadors presenting their *lettres de créance*, patron-saint receptions, the dictator's daughter's wedding. The guerrillas fired at the palace guards even before they got out of the cars. But in the *plan de ataque* they had failed to include the café on the corner, where soldiers from the garrison would often eat and drink. Alerted by the shots they really became a devastating surprise rear guard: the surprisers taken by surprise. Fortunately (though they couldn't use that word) that was when the rest of the cars arrived.

For their own protection all the insurgents were armed only with handguns and a few hand grenades they could hide in their pockets. The van of the Fastaction Dry-cleaners ('We deliver'), full of rifles M1 and submachine guns and ammunition, remained parked on a side street of the palace, waiting for the support group to come. They never came. Moreover, the men in charge of taking the building of the Fine Arts Museum, right across the small square, to neutralize from its roof the machine gun on the palace roof (the museum was taller than the palace) they never came either. They failed to do so or came too late or got lost. Whatever. Nevertheless the men at the back gate managed to kill all the guards and forced their way into the palace. Some even got up to the top floors – to find that the map of the building, which they had studied for months and even memorized, was incomplete: the old floor plan did not include the recent refurbishment ordered by the dictator. Among the changes there was a secret lift which went from the president's offices to the roof, where he had decreed the building of an apparently impregnable annexe. The lift was bullet-proof too.

Because the hand grenades, evidently obsolete, did not explode, rolling inertly like stones into any odd corner, two bold attackers forced their way to the first floor with handguns only. Somehow they reached the presidential office – which was empty of course. Just at that very moment the telephone on the desk with the President's Seal rang incongruously. One of the guerrillas, he whose name was Peligro, incomprehensibly picked up the receiver (why did he do it?) to hear a woman's voice utterly garbled. She talked in a Spanish so thick that he almost didn't understand what she was trying to say. It was a call from New York by a woman journalist. She asked if it was true that they had stormed the palace, the *presidential* palace? The guerrilla said it was true: the dictator's den had been successfully attacked. He identified himself as one of the insurgents. The woman journalist wanted to know if el Señor Presidente was dead or alive. The guerrilla said: 'The tyrant is dead' and then hung up. It was a political lie but those were also his last words. As he was leaving the empty office rifle-fire from the other end of

91

the palace killed him instantly. His comrade made a hasty retreat down the staircase.

The only thing left for the remaining assaulters to do now was to get out of the building the best way they could – if they could. It was of course more difficult to abandon the presidential palace than to storm it. Much more difficult in fact than it had been to plan Operation Sic Semper Tyrannis: so successful on paper, so disastrously carried out. The political group that conceived it, the second in importance of the clandestine opposition, was virtually wiped out: they lost ninety per cent of their men in the operation. You couldn't spell it in so many words then because they were all martyrs but it was all a mess.

The dictator, after getting thousands of congratulatory messages for just being alive, remained in power for three more years. Other guerrilla groups won the war in the mountains, long after they had decided that the assault on the presidential palace was a bad idea after all. They were right but one could say that in the suicide mission heroism and failure had been joined to make it memorable. It was in fact folly in reverse.

HE CAME WITH THE OTHER PRISONERS in single file through the gates flanked by policemen wielding rifles. That's how they left the prison: one by one they climbed into the vans and were taken to the courthouse escorted by three patrol cars. They considered the custody escape-proof.

They entered the Palace of Justice, where in spots you could see the old stone, which the rain and not time had stripped of its yellow paint and plaster. Some of the prisoners wore dark glasses and were blinded for a moment in the dark interior, which contrasted by design with the sunlight outside. Footsteps could be heard now in the trial room. Relatives and lawyers and newsmen were crowding the rooms and curious bystanders were hanging around in the hallways.

When going from the entrance-way and the corridor into the courtyard where, during the recesses, people would stand around talking, the line of prisoners (dressed in the prison's uniform: blue trousers and blue shirt and blue cap which now they held in their hands out of respect for the Law), demons in denim, they turned to the left to gather in the waiting room to wait before the law. It was then that the thin pale boy without dark glasses left the line sidestepping to go into one of the empty rooms where only ghosts were expecting justice to be done. He hid behind the heavy door and waited. When they had all passed by, prisoners and policemen, he took off his uniform shirt to show that beneath it he was wearing another shirt with red and green palm trees in a white landscape (or the other way round), which he pulled out to cover part of his prison pants. He threw the blue shirt and cap in a corner behind the door and put on sunglasses before going out into the hallway. Calmly he crossed the

93

courtyard, went out on the street through the main door and hailed a taxi to make his getaway.

The next morning the newspapers published photographs of the blue shirt, jail denim, and the cap, now black or grey, and a sketch of the supposed route of escape which looked more like a blueprint of a labyrinth: here's where you get in, here's where you get away. In fact, the idea had come to the pale young man that very morning. He had wanted to put it into practice immediately and there was in its simplicity a genial touch of luck which made it a success. But there was no master plan, no escape maps or plots. In one word, no maze – though it was of course amazing.

LATE AT NIGHT, milk-trucks crisscross the city. At dawn it seems that the streets, the city, belong to them. They cross the avenues and the side streets at the same speed, without stopping and often without their lights on. But one of them is not a milk-truck. Perhaps it's the most cautious one, going slowly, with lights on, and making signals at each side street. Perhaps it's that one, drawn by a horse, which crosses the city from twelve to six. Nobody knows a thing. They all talk about the milk-truck, but nobody knows for sure. They say it comes out of the cellar of a police station and carries inside a corpse – or two or three, whatever's around. The corpse is always a former prisoner of the opposition and if he was lucky they killed him right away. Others are tortured first, and their relatives have a hard time trying to recognize them at the morgue.

THE PLANES DROPPED BOMBS AT SUNRISE. One bomb fell on a hovel and killed a family, another fell on the hospital, which had already been evacuated. The shelters withstood it, but after the attack they were full of dirt, pieces of wood and rubbish. The term 'air-raid shelter' suggests the military stability of a bunker or the civil security of a cellar or the tube, but these shelters were primitive and brought to mind something more like a cross between a cave and a log cabin. They were constructed in gulches or in dry riverbeds, or sometimes beside hills. The hills were the walls and the roofs were made of thick wooden piles tied with rope or rattan, and lastly, everything was covered with dirt and stones, and if possible, mud. They were, all in all, good shelter against shrapnel and if they didn't receive a direct hit they could be considered secure – though few air-raid shelters offer protection against direct impact.

There were dead and wounded rebels. Among the wounded was a communications sergeant, a blond boy with a sparse beard who looked like a peasant. He had remained behind to establish contact with command headquarters, and a bomb exploded near by. He was wounded in the side and as the wound was small, the doctor decided to attend to it last. But now he was on the ground, holding the wound with his hands and screaming, howling with pain. The comandante heard him and came quickly. He stooped over the wounded man and said, between his teeth: Goddammit, what kind of man are you? Take it like a man, it's nothing, he said, and he took the boy's hand away from his stomach, looked at the wound and appraised it, clicking his tongue. Shit, that's only a scratch, he said, and you're scaring the wounded civilians.

Goddammit. Don't forget that you're a soldier! he said, and got up and walked away. The boy bit his tongue, his lips, and saliva ran down one side of his mouth. He didn't say anything; he couldn't speak. He dug his hands into the earth, sinking his fingers in the grass, in the dirt. When the comandante had spoken to him, he was red in the face; now he was very pale.

When the doctor came, he was dying. The doctor called to the comandante but it was useless, because he had gone into a coma and his agony was brief. The doctor turned over the corpse and saw that the wound had no exit, and so he decided to do an autopsy. The comandante helped him. The wound could barely be seen inside the viscera and the doctor took out a fistful of faeces and among them, shining in the sun, six, ten, twelve sharp grey nasty little pieces of shrapnel: a splinter had hit him, splitting up in the intestinal cavity as it entered, forming a shower of swift razors which perforated his intestines and burst his liver. Technically he was dead from the start, the doctor said.

The comandante wiped the blood off his hands with a rag, which he threw away. He took off his hat and walked to the radio post under the tree, and when he got there he kicked the tree.

HE CAME WALKING DOWN THE SIDEWALK, going right past the police colonel's mansion, and he entered the house next door, still carrying his parcel. When he was in the room he gave the parcel to his host and said to him: 'Here's the dynamite. Put it in a safe place – and be careful, it might give you a headache. My head is splitting right now.' His host brought him an aspirin and finally the young terrorist lay down on his bed in the room where he'd been hiding for six months now. They put the dynamite in a closet in the room where his parents and his eldest daughter slept. About an hour later, the other terrorist came to call for the borrowed dynamite. He was very nervous and when he left the house he hesitated a moment before going out on the sidewalk.

IS IT TRUE that no plough stops for a dying man? The cars passed by the whole night while the man was dying on one side of the highway. They must have taken him out of prison at midnight and killed him here. Or maybe he was dead, tortured to death, and a truck brought him at dawn and left him beside the little lake. Or they threw him, at nightfall, from a patrol car. They left him for dead but the man was still alive and was dying the whole night long.

Dawn came, as always. The moon was hidden early and Venus first became more luminous and then paler, fainter. The land breeze had stopped, but it was cooler than it had been at sunset. Several roosters crowed or one rooster crowed several times. The birds began to whistle or to chirp or to warble, without stirring from the trees. The sky became blue and then returned to violet, then purple, red, pink, and later orange and yellow and white, as the sun came up. The clouds came from the coast. Now you could smell coffee. Someone opened an iron gate. The traffic became heavier.

The body remained in the gutter until mid-morning, when the coroner picked it up. Brueghel was right after all.

HIS SPRINGFIELD RESTS AGAINST A TREE. The other man, luckier or older, has a Garand rifle at his feet. It's midday and they're sitting under a *ceiba* tree, taking advantage of the shade and the breeze to complete the manoeuvres. The two are bearded and long-haired, but one is wearing a palm-leaf hat and the other a baseball cap, and on each of their shoulders, comandantes' stars are embroidered over the red-and-black triangle. The younger one chews an extinguished cigar and looks attentively at the checkered mat before him: he seems to be studying it. The older one pulls on his dusty beard and smiles. There's a breeze now and the papers on the table rise in an attempt to fly, but their airborne rebellion is futile against the tyranny of stone paperweights. The young man is thinking perhaps about tactics – certain flank manoeuvres, maybe a sudden attack. The old man seems to have faith in ambushes, in a raid guaranteed by the protection of night and surprise. Further away, the rebels chat in the grass or clean their rifles, or sleep in the open air: it's not any business of theirs; let the comandantes decide. The two leaders are concentrating on the strategic operations board and they brood in silence. The old man takes off his hat and wipes the sweat off his forehead with his sleeve. Now it's the young man who smiles and offers a tactical solution. The old man wants to protest, but says nothing: he knows that war requires courage and also prudence.

They've been at it for an hour, an hour and a half, two hours, and nobody dares to interrupt them, because they all realize it's a historic moment. The shade of the tree has moved and the paper seems stained by the light and the shadows. The old man offers his hand, laughs, and announces, 'Checkmate, pal,' in a victorious voice.

HE WAS A COUNTRY DOCTOR BY CHOICE. He was young, handsome and rich. At least he arrived in town driving a brand-new jeep and his wife owned a Pontiac convertible. He was tall, blond and blue-eyed. His wife, though also young, was rather homely. But he didn't seem to show any interest in the local beauties. So why had such a gifted doctor come to pitch tent in a poor country town, almost a village? Surely a brilliant future was in wait for him in Havana. Some people couldn't understand that if the times were brutish and nasty the new doctor was an altruist. He really loved the poor. More often than not he wouldn't charge for his services, especially if the patient was a peasant. 'Some other time', was his verbal prescription in most cases. He was with the dictatorship all right but he was all right. He loved the General but you could trust him.

Suddenly there was one of those reversals of fortune that fate enjoys performing.

Two rebels assaulted the town barracks – a futile gesture if ever there was one. One of the attackers was killed and the other was badly wounded. They in turn had killed the captain of the garrison and a useless old soldier everybody knew in town as an amiable crank. The wounded youth (he was barely twenty) came to the doctor's house by sheer chance. One must believe that he didn't even see the brass plaque on the doctor's door. Fate is such a grim joker!

He had life enough to knock on the door. He was admitted by the doctor himself (his wife was not in) and collapsed in his arms. The critically wounded stranger would surely die in such a small town, the doctor diagnosed, and he was not a surgeon. There was nothing he could do except perhaps to take him to the hospital in the nearest city, which was called Sancti Spiritus. That it was named after the Holy Ghost was not at all ironical. The doctor helped his patient to his car and drove away and on to the direct route to the city. The doctor never arrived and the young incompetent rebel never made it. Someone in town saw the doctor taking the wounded terrorist into his jeep and squealed to the local police. As usual the telephone was faster. The doctor was intercepted by the political police on the outskirts of the city. His patient was luckier than the doctor for he died of his wounds as he was brutally pushed out of the car. The doctor was tortured by the police with precise but not refined sadism: they pulled out his fingernails first, they plucked his eyes as if they were eyebrows. When they finally moved him to the hospital (he was heading for it when he left town) he was already dead. None of his friends could have recognized the good old doctor.

THE CHAPLAIN WAS A PRIEST who came to the mountains like many other guerrilla fighters. He wasn't defrocked, but he drank. For a long time his favourite drink was the brandy Tres Medallas, advertised on radio with a jingle that ended in the words 'Let Three Medals accompany you'. It was popularly known as Three Mellows. The chaplain continued drinking in the sierra and sometimes had problems, though everyone admired his courage and the way he carried his liquor.

Once they caught the leader of a group of bandidos and they sentenced him to death. The bandit said that he was Catholic and requested a priest to give him absolution. They called the chaplain, who came, stood next to the outlaw and said to him, *'Ego te absolvo in nomine Patris et Filii et Spiritus Sancti.'* The bandit complained that he didn't know any foreign languages and that he wanted absolution in Spanish. The chaplain lowered and raised his head twice and said to him, 'Well, my son: Let Three Medals accompany you.' They all laughed, even the outlaw, who had always bragged that he never knew fear.

SOMEONE ONCE SAID that young men don't think about death.

This boy was sitting on the protruding roots of a *jagüey* and eating a mango. The juice stained his black beard and ran down his hands. He was laughing, because next to him another rebel was telling a story. The thing is, the storyteller said, the nephew was, you know, kind of dumb. But there was nobody else around to give his aunt the shot, so he had to do it. The others laughed. They knew the story but they laughed. So the nephew goes to the drugstore and comes back with the medicine and the syringe and gets it all ready so that he can give his aunt the shot, and she had to pick up her petticoats, and then he asks her, just like this, with his dumb face, Hey, Aunt, where do I put it, in the hole or in the slit?

He lurched backward, exaggerating his happiness, but really happy, with the mango stone in his mouth, squeezing the stringy flesh between his teeth. He saw the branches of the *jagüey* swaying and crossing each other in the sky, and when they moved the sun appeared and disappeared among the leaves, making the trees and the branches and the landscape white. He closed his eyes and saw red and black and red again. He laughed and heard the wind in the trees and the creaking of the branches and a bird singing – no: chirping. Maybe a Cuban watchbird: the peasants call it that because of its sound, without knowing why, though they explain by saying that it's useful because it always chirps when it sees a man come near, and the peasants and other birds and the wild animals on the island use it was a watchbird. The rebels were using it as their own watch too.

He laughed, closing his eyes, the mango in his hand,

his arms up high, covered with yellow right up to the olive green of his sleeve, stretching them out to gain his balance and maybe to stand up. He was laughing when the shot knocked him down. He never knew what killed him, a stray bullet from one of his comrades or a shot from an enemy ambush or what. He fell to one side and rolled from the tree down toward the ravine. What was he thinking? Someone once said that we never know what the brave man thinks.

ONE OF THE HEAD COMANDANTE'S HABITS, when he'd captured a badly wounded soldier, was to make himself out to be the soldier's friend. He'd come near the dying man, whisper in his ear and make the man trust him, so that he could get information on the enemy, and the comandante wouldn't let anybody, not even the medics, come near the wounded man until he got what he wanted – or until the soldier died. This custom always revolted the other comandante.

ALTHOUGH THE THREE OF THEM ARE LYING IN THE GRASS, it's not *Le Déjeuner sur l'herbe*. One has a hole in his forehead, another hole in his face, and a third hole in his neck. The other one is face down and there's something wrong with his head. Perhaps it was beaten or shot up. The third one, a shirtless mulatto, received at least ten shots in his chest and stomach. In the foreground you can see a strip of asphalt which must be the highway, and behind it a segment of beach or the coast, the sea.

They don't move because it's a photograph and because they've been dead for hours and were left near the highway as a warning.

ANCIENT FABLES seem improbable and the moral lesson is always useless: it only happens to the animals in the fables, and the experience belongs to someone else's life. In modern fables the characters are different, and this one, told all over, features a didactic father and an empty-headed son. The father wanted to teach his son a lesson and to offer some advice that would be prophetic: like all preachers, he aspired to become a seer. One day a friend suggested a cure and the man followed his advice.

He invited the chief of police to lunch and the guest regarded his host's request as a great joke. It was to catch the prodigal son (whose only interest was drinking and women and night-life) on his rounds, accuse him of being a terrorist leader and lock him in a cell. The next morning he would certainly be, as the ads for a fashionable antacid pill said, completely cured.

The young man did not get over his amazement, nor did he get out of jail. Imprisoned at the precinct, protesting his innocence, he was left in the charge of the captain with a wink from the chief. The son and that criminally exemplary Polonius who was his father ran into a streak of bad luck: the captain went out to eat with his mistress, and that night ten political bombs exploded and the Ministry of the Interior decreed the death of one hostage per bomb: any prisoner in the first ten precincts. He was in the third or seventh and he didn't wake up with his tongue raspy from drink nor with a hangover nor with a woman at his side: he simply didn't wake up.

The moral is that the times made the fable not only believable, but also possible.

HE HAD A MEAN, AWKWARD, and sometimes, like now, a ferocious face. They shot him under a tree. The trial lasted fifteen minutes. Charges: robbery, rape and desertion; perhaps he had also passed information to the enemy. The public prosecutor was the comandante and he trembled when he spoke, saying: This man who you see here (pointing: he left his forefinger like that the whole time of the trial) is evil and you shouldn't feel any pain for him. Pain *he* deserves, a lot of pain, the pain of death many times over. Since we can only kill him once, I ask that he be sentenced immediately and that we not waste many bullets on him. The defence lawyer (a captain, who was named against the will of the accused, who didn't want any defence, and who spoke very rapidly) said that there were no possible extenuating circumstances for the crimes imputed to and, indeed, committed by the defendant, but nevertheless he appealed to rebel justice that he be sentenced to a firing squad and not be killed with one shot in the back of the head like a mad dog he said that they should remember his courage in the past he said that the desertion had not taken place and that there was no evidence of his being an informer he said for all of which he also demanded the death sentence, but by the firing squad. They shot him right there and then, against the *arabo* tree under whose shade the trial took place: only the judges had to vacate the premises. Before dying, the outlaw asked a question. Comandante, he said, how should I stand: facing them or with my back turned? You, facing them, said the head comandante. He asked to command the firing squad but he wasn't allowed.

THE COMANDANTE WALKED DOWN THE MIDDLE OF THE STREET in the dark. It hadn't rained for days, but whether or not he raised dust as he walked he didn't know. He could barely hear the creaking of the big boots of the captain who walked invisibly beside him. They were headed for the army barracks. In guerrilla warfare a comandante has to be minister of war, master strategist, commanding officer, colonel of a chosen regiment, storm trooper, and even scout. Tonight he was a wandering scout. The regiment (or should one say the rest of them?) were surrounding the barracks and waiting for the signal to attack, a shot.

Although it was a hot night out, a light breeze was blowing now which moved the dust in the direction of the barracks. It was not yet nine but the town was asleep, lifeless, and if it had been another comandante, he would have thought of the ghost towns in westerns. But this comandante didn't like the movies.

They turned into the main street and almost bumped into a soldier, who automatically said halt. The comandante had his Thompson cocked. (Before continuing, it would be a good idea to give a biography of this weapon. During the early days of the struggle in the mountains, the comandante, who was not yet comandante, had won it in a battle. When he first saw it, it was travelling in a small army truck. The truck, blown sky-high by a land mine, fell on top of the Thompson and it was never the same – the machine gun, not the truck. At times, when it was most needed, it refused to work. Most probably it was an excessively loyal weapon and still felt it was with the enemy.) When the comandante saw that the soldier, also ready, was about to shoot, he pulled the trigger.

Nothing doing: not a shot, not a sound, not even a click. The captain realized what was happening and remembered the history of the reluctant Thompson: it's curious how many things one can think of (and do) in seconds. This man (who was carrying a shotgun, an old friend of the family, you might say: it had belonged to his grandfather, who fought in the brief second war of independence) also tried to shoot, but the shotgun copied the machine gun and jammed as if in a sympathy strike. The captain later thought that, after all, it was a weapon that had been in the house too long, employed in occasional hunting, and that it would naturally react with this untimely pacifism at the eleventh hour.

The only weapon that worked was the soldier's rifle. The comandante did what any other human being (except, maybe, General Custer) would have done. He ran; he ran as he had never run or thought he could run and he himself later told that as he ran he wondered how many records he was breaking that night. The captain, who was second in command, was now first, since he took off before his comandante. It seems that everyone ran that time, because the bullets didn't reach human flesh, and after the garrison had surrendered (the shots from the Garand were taken for the signal for the attack, which didn't last more than a half hour) they found the trembling soldier crouched behind a column in a nearby colonnade, and his rifle in the middle of a dusty street.

The comandante was fair. He gave the rifle to the captain (who kept the old shotgun so that his son or grandson could hunt in peacetime, certain that there would never be a hunting accident in the house) and he found in the barracks a Browning machine gun, which he kept for the rest of the war – a neutral weapon which always fired when its present master pulled the trigger, without wondering whom it was killing or maiming.

IN GRIMMER DAYS the chief of police in Havana was called Pilar. Believe it or not this is a girl's name everywhere in the Spanish-speaking world. But the policeman named with a woman's name was no woman and the *habaneros* knew it. He was the dictatorship's last resort to pacify a city that had become a hotbed of terror. Because he was known as a tough enforcer the dictator personally brought him over from Matanzas, where he had been a colonel, to become chief of police in Havana, the city that never wept, with the rank of general.

Then in what was a *ci-devant* enclave called the Zone of Sin in Zulueta Street (from the Sloppy Joe's Bar to the Dirty Dick's Tavern: between the dark and the colonnade) there was a strident strife that the press called a raging to-do the next day. It happened late at night and the police arrived in stealth in patrol cars and Black Marias. They completed the raid by apprehending what they identified over the radio as a 'bunch of perverts'. At the time the streets of Havana after dark were peopled only by terrorists, policemen and gays. The gays were in fact a third force. The General knew it; many policemen knew it too. But now they just rounded up every gay in the bars as if they were all the usual suspects in a movie about Nazis and the Resistance.

When he found it out early next morning, General Pilar was truly furious and called the captain of the third precinct with such a loud voice that he didn't even need a phone. 'Who the hell gave you any orders to gather the gays!' The captain tried some lame excuse by stammering. 'Don't you know goddammit', said General Pilar still shouting, 'that the gays are the only gaiety left in town?' The captain tried to smile. 'I don't want any of you guys to touch the gays even with a night stick, you hear?' He made a pause to cool off: 'Unless, of course, you have gays in uniform and they want to do some touching of their own.' The captain couldn't help laughing. 'Don't you make my gays so sad that they disappear from the streets at night,' he stated. 'Those gays are wanted, but not the way you mean.'

General Pilar, you've just witnessed it, had a sense of humour. Nevertheless he was a cruel cop with the terrorists and when the government fell just a few months after he became top cop in Havana he had to leave the island in a hurry. Never trust a cop who banters. Remember that a joke is closer to a yoke than you think.

THE COMANDANTE DRAWS A BATTLE PLAN in the dust. He puts a lot of care into its execution, great precision in the assigning of posts, he makes an exact calculation of the enemy's capability and of all the pros and cons. But in the end, the battle is won by mere chance or by the reluctant initiative of two or three brave men who didn't understand the explanations at all, who don't know anything about anything, who can't distinguish between strategy and tactics – who don't even know these words.

ONLY TWO MEN came with the three hundred prisoners, the doctor and a medic, and neither was armed. They began their descent at dawn and at five in the afternoon they reached the village. Many of them were wounded and those who couldn't walk were carried on stretchers by their comrades. (In the field hospital there were still some critically wounded left.) There were soldiers and officers. The highest-ranking prisoner was a captain with a leg wound, who insisted upon walking down the mountain. The medic made him a walking stick and from afar, tall, erect, excessively proud, he looked like a field marshal with his staff. They stopped to rest at noon and the doctor and the medic handed out crackers and guava paste and water. Some soldiers helped them.

At first they had thought of sending an escort, but then they saw that there weren't enough men and they decided on this formula. One of the comandantes insisted that it was risky, that there would be a mutiny or that maybe the doctors [*sic*] would end up prisoners. None of that happened. It appeared a strange procession, the bearded soldiers (one or two; the captain and the other officers insisted upon shaving, but the troops, maybe out of laziness or a twisted sense of humour, let their beards grow) coming down the hills, with the bearded doctor in his rebel uniform and the beardless medic, his long hair tied in a ponytail, also in olive green, both at the rear.

They reached town, found the Red Cross people and immediately made their delivery. The army medical officers, when they arrived, saluted them, clicking their heels. They also saluted but were too tired to click their boots together. Besides, they didn't know how to do it properly.

AT FIRST THEY DIDN'T TAKE HIM SERIOUSLY. He was the doctor, OK, but too refined, and in any case, his hands were much too delicate for war. But then, when he showed that he could go up and down the mountains like everybody else, and when he reached the mountain top before anybody else and wasn't out of breath, and when bombs were dropping and everybody was desperately burrowing into the dirt for shelter and he continued doing a transfusion, then they began to have more respect for him and they stopped calling him Doc and instead called him Captain or (some of them) Captain, sir.

But that music he always looked for on the radio, especially at night: funeral parlour music, music for the dead. (It's also true that the radio was his and that he always lent it out and that others had it more than he.)

One day, one evening, as the sun turned pink, dark red, purple, mauve, and he left on the radio a popular tune, a cha-cha-cha or something like that, a tall, strong, Indian-looking, slow-talking rebel came over, left his rifle against the side of the hut (the battlefield hospital) and said: Hey, Doc, I didn't know you liked the hot stuff. What? he said. I didn't know, Captain, said the other, that you liked real music, the hot stuff, he said. Since you listen to that funeral music all the time. The doctor looked at him and smiled. I like *all* good music, he said. You're the one who's missing a part of the good stuff. Yeah? the other said. What d'you mean by that? Come over here whenever you can, said the doctor, and listen. From then on he tried to tame the beast inside the soldier with sonatas, concertos, symphonies, but the music therapy didn't last long. It's difficult to play *Pygmalion* in the middle of a war: a bullet or an order can destroy the best

Galatea. This rebel didn't die; they sent him to head-quarters up in the mountains and the only music he listened to there was the song of the mockingbird in the morning, the wind whistling through the branches, and the screeching of the crickets at night.

Every day the doctor would surprise the recruits (the hospital was in the rear, near the military school) by shaving early in the morning. He was the only officer who didn't wear a beard. He shocked newcomers and veterans when one day he insisted upon going to the city to have a wisdom tooth pulled because he didn't trust the arts of the rebel dentist. He went despite advice and disobeyed an order from his superior. He didn't go on the journey dressed as a peasant, because his manners and hands would have betrayed him. He disguised himself as a foreign geologist and spent hours perfecting an imaginary accent. He reached the city at noon and went straight to the dentist's house. Before arriving, he slowed down and when he entered the street he adopted incredibly extreme precautions. He reached the door, looked at the sign and put his hand on the knocker without knocking. He took his hand off the knocker, went across the street, came back. He looked once more at the name on the bronze sign and raised his hand to his face and felt his tooth under the skin. It doesn't hurt any more, he said. How strange. He made sure with his tongue that it was the bad tooth and he was right. How strange, it's all right, he said. It seems that the journey took the pain away. I'd better not have it pulled out, then. It's a healthy wisdom tooth, he said, and he returned to the mountains without waiting for his escort, who was to come for him at a certain time.

HE'S FALLING, BEHIND THE HILL: the grey arm raised without anger against the white sky where there's a whiter sun which you now can't see, the grey hand, the dark-grey forearm, the black rifle next to, stuck to, fused with the pale-grey chest with the black stain on one side, without pain or surprise because they didn't give him time, without knowing that he's falling on the black grass, without ever knowing that they'll see him fall again and again, like this, he hasn't yet fallen but he is falling because a black shoulder, the black-grey-black pants (there's no longer any colour, no olive-green uniform nor red-and-black band nor blue eyes: all hues depend on the eternal, levelling sunlight), the grey neck, the grey-grey face, the whole grey-black left side is going, fading, vanishing, leaning toward the black earth and death for ever: the volley or the single shot wasn't heard but the impact is felt and he will fall as long as man exists and they will see him falling without ever falling when eyes look at him and they will not forget him as long as there is memory.

THE MAN WAS CALLED EL HOMBRE by his followers, but he was just a greedy dictator who happened to trigger a revolution. He didn't know it when he decided to flee instead of fighting it out with a guerrilla group outnumbered ten to one by his army equipped with the most modern weapons. It would have been as easy to wipe them out in the countryside as he had done in the cities. But he decided to leave the country, 'So as to avoid any more bloodshed from the innocent and the young'. That's what he said when he chose New Year's Eve to make his getaway, for he was also a thief and had to protect his loot. The traditional New Year's ball at the officers' club would mask his escape. This time only generals and colonels were invited to the party within the party. There was also his chief of police, the mayor of Havana, several ministers (though not all), the head of the navy and assorted friends.

At twelve o'clock midnight, or perhaps a few minutes before, there was a slight confusion among the chosen to board the ark – or rather arks. Some exalted soldiers shouted, *'Viva el General!'*, some sang the national anthem a cappella. After a hurried toast the dictator crashed his champagne glass on the floor. So did his closest minions. Suddenly there was a din louder than the breaking of glass and the dictator knew it was time for him to depose himself. *'Pancho, mi viejo'* he shouted at his Old Faithful, the chief of staff of the army. As agreed, military planes would take him, would take them all in fact, to a nearby island. Over there he should see what he should see: the USA so reluctant then, Europe, Spain maybe? He had to hurry now. His air force was not his any more even though the pilots still obeyed his orders. One must go aboard in perfect calm and order. Should one wave a handkerchief or just the hand? Goodbye, goodbye! The planes began to take off in the general direction of the sunrise to fly over Oriente province, where all this nasty affair began. Then towards the Dominican Republic, where an older dictator will be welcoming him to plunder most of his loot. Anyway, sitting in his seat the general, who fancied himself as a military man above all, was very pleased with a retreat completed in so orderly a fashion. He had code-named the fugitive gathering Operation We Shall Return. Did he really believe it?

IT HAPPENED JUST BEFORE REVEILLE. They were still in bed. She looked languid in his strong brown arms. She was in fact the mix-up as before and the young lieutenant was having problems with his foreplay. But now she seemed to be yielding. That's a good girl, he thought, though she was no longer a girl. Obviously he couldn't realize how tired, how terribly tired she was after the Farewell to the Year Ball. Actually she had tried to say not tonight darling but it was no use. He was laying siege to her. Soldiers all. Suddenly she pricked up her lovely ears, lovat diamonds in her lobes, listening to a loud noise. There was a terrible thunder somewhere beyond the widow, *window*. It sounded more like cannon-fire than a storm warning. She was alarmed. 'Listen, listen,' the livid lady whispered in her lover's mouth. 'What?' He expected a low confession, the heralding of a coitus less reservatus perhaps. Then she was almost sitting in bed, practically slipping away from him. 'That noise.' 'What (in hell he thought but said:) noise, dear?' He was flustered, feeling that either ardour or ado, something, had got to give. 'That distant din,' she said, gesturing vaguely at some point of support. '*¿No oyes?*' and then 'Can't you hear?' He was past hearing and dismissed her with a joke: 'Oh, don't pay any attention to it, *rica*. It's only the government falling.' He had heard that joke in the barracks before but this time it wasn't a joke.

IN THE PHOTOGRAPH YOU CAN SEE THE COMANDANTE-IN-CHIEF entering the capital in a jeep. Next to him is another comandante and you can see the driver and another member of the escort. In the background the crowd cheers the heroes. But the photographer had a touch of foresight. As he didn't know the third comandante, he cut him out of the picture when cropping it. A few months later the third comandante was in jail, accused of treason and sentenced to thirty years in prison. All those who had anything to do with him were immediately branded as suspects, and the historians proceeded to erase his name from the books. Ahead of his time, the photographer did not have to look for his photograph to cut it accordingly. That's what you call historical guesswork.

IT IS NOT A PHOTOGRAPH THIS TIME but a film and not a very good one at that. It is all grey and scratchy and jumpy, probably taken with a sixteen-millimetre camera, shot by a cameraman from the newsreels with more guts than eyes. But the sound is all right. On the screen you can see an old soldier (he is balding, with white hair) briefly standing not against the traditional wall called *paredón* in the Spanish-speaking world, but on the edge of a trench. They had dug it behind him as a grave into which he will be pushed by the volley. But at least it is not a mass grave. He is, or rather was, a general of the dictatorship's army. He was brave and loyal and the dictator paid him back by leaving him behind without even saying goodbye on the telephone. But now he is calmly addressing himself to a shooting squad we won't see because they chose to remain, like a shy director, behind a camera that is somewhat askew.

'Well *muchachos*,' said the general in a loud voice but in a genial vein. 'I leave you with your revolution.' He uttered his last words as if he were just an after-dinner speaker: 'I hope you enjoy it.'

All of a sudden the man disappears from the screen as in any tricky old movie by Melies.

THEY MADE HIM A COMANDANTE AT TWENTY-THREE and he joked about the black general of the wars of independence who was made a major-general *before* thirty. 'Those were the days,' he sighed half in jest, half in earnest. He was master executioner in Las Villas province and he commanded the firing squad that shot the general who delivered a speech to the film crew before he was erased by the volley. He gave the general his personal *tiro de gracia*. He then moved into the house of the dead general when his grieving family had not yet moved out. He felt like a lord but he was a modest young man and didn't proclaim it. He said instead that he felt like a lord's son. But he was merely a usurper. He loved the spacious country house and between assignments (an execution here, a chase after what the government called *bandidos* there) he found his house an abode fit for a general.

But one night his mansion started to creak and to squeak and even to crack and his mother told him when he came back that the house was haunted. 'Haunted my foot!' he said and as he loved to roam the house barefoot like a peasant he wiggled his big toe at his mother. 'See? I have a haunted foot.' But his mother didn't laugh: she was certain that the house that once belonged to the dead general was now haunted. One day his terrified mother left the house never to come back. She didn't even take her clothes with her. The house could be haunted but he was undaunted. He said that superstitions belong in the past. 'And we've killed the past.'

One night he gave a dinner for his fellow officers and he told them about the haunted house. 'They say,' he said, 'that my house is haunted by the former son of a bitch but I am now the present son of a bitch.' They smiled

124

politely: even executioners can be polite. 'I'll hunt the haunter,' he promised. He drew his big Colt .45 revolver, the biggest gun in the province, aimed at the dark and took a vow. 'I killed the bastard son of a bitch once and I'm ready to kill him again.' They all laughed now though it was not funny. But he wanted to be large in mirth, so they laughed again though there was no joke. They went on eating and drinking rum, the last of the Bacardi. 'Fill full,' he begged. 'I drink to the general,' he said and then stopped.

By midnight all the guests were drunk and sleepy. They fell asleep at table, their heads on the table, beards and long hair all over the plates. But he wasn't asleep. He was in fact waiting for another guest. He was expecting the *comandante en jefe* to come, as he always did, between midnight and the crack of dawn. The chief was always late as it was his wont, but he always came when he said he'd come. But instead of the comandante the dead general came to visit his house as the ghost his mother saw. He too saw it now. He looked like the general all right. He even had blood coming from his head wounds. He didn't look dead, yet not alive. He was an undead now. Was he, the young executioner, afraid of the dead? 'I never shake,' he said aloud. 'It's the table that moved.' But nobody heard him. Then, all of a sudden, he drew his gun again and fired at the shade. He couldn't kill it because he had already killed him. He fired more shots. His guests woke up. Suddenly there was a great alarm among them. They saw him, gun in hand, and demanded an explanation. He didn't have any: he only babbled incoherencies about ghosts and dead generals. Apparently a general from the past regime had come into the room earlier in the night. But he seemed to have disappeared now. They decided he was either a liar or gun-crazy. Out of fear they never came to his parties again but the ghost did, every night. Some time later he shot himself with his Colt gun. His cronies decided that he *was* crazy. Gun-crazy.

THE SECOND COMANDANTE disappeared in the plane that was taking him back to the capital after he had put the third comandante in prison. The comandante-in-chief went off in the presidential plane to look for him. But the plane made a cursory tour and the head comandante went to see the cows and bulls at a requisitoned ranch. At night he watched television and went to bed late, fascinated by the noisy adventures of a cowboy and a bunch of Indians. The next morning he returned to the capital, not without first making another cursory tour of the area where the second comandante had disappeared. As the plane landed, the head comandante saw the second comandante's parents waiting anxiously. Until that moment the comandante-in-chief had been joking and talking trivia, but when he saw the anxious couple he suddenly looked remorseful and went up to them to embrace them in condolence. Tears almost came to his eyes.

THE PHOTOGRAPH IS AN ICON, which doesn't always happen with photographs. The comandante is standing firmly on his two feet, in an 'at ease' stance. The position is military, but also Cuban and very personal, with the legs apart, and the breeze rippling his baggy pants. His hands rest one on top of the other over the mouth of his rifle: a Garand, or a Springfield, or maybe an old Spanish Mauser. That war had been fought with all available weapons, some unconventional, perhaps even prohibited by the Geneva Convention: bamboo cannons, oil-barrel mines and shotguns filled with pebbles. The comandante's usual cowboy boots can't be seen. Behind him are some bushes that look like *vicarias*, very pleasant and serene garden plants which you often see in country cemeteries. But he's not in the cemetery because the comandante liked living things. Behind the *vicarias* there's a wooden house. You can't see any doors or windows, just rough boards: it's a house in a country town or in the suburbs. The comandante wears an old, worn, open shirt, without a tie, with a band on his left arm which says '2 of Ju— ' and you can't read anything further. From his neck hangs a striped scarf that falls over his chest. He sports the famous beard and long hair and a Texan stetson which he always wore tipped back. His mouth is serious, but by his eyes you can see he's amused by the picture-taking and by the faces of those looking at it – even those reading this inventory now. His outfit is completed by a wide belt (with a large, square metal buckle), from which a sheathed hunter's knife hangs, along with two cartridge clips, for his pistol on the left and the Browning in its holster on the right. The large pockets of his combat pants are full, as always, of grenades, pencil butts, pieces of paper and candy, in that order. Behind, over his head, like an irreverent halo, there's an inscription (in pencil, probably on the original of this photo, this being a copy) written in wild letters, saying: 'Cheo Prado Photos'. Since Cheo Prado revealed his genius as a photographer here and didn't want to remain anonymous (Cheo Prado is an artist and not a pioneer: more Cartier-Bresson than Niepce), he is nearly eponymous now.

The comandante is dead today and the same shortcomings and virtues that transformed him, in six months, from a shopkeeper to a warrior and an expert in guerrilla warfare and a strategist, also killed him, in his full glory, like the ancient heroes. In the photo you can see his gallantry, his courage, his poise, his unlimited confidence in himself, his disbelief of death, and at the same time you can see that within him there was always a skirt-chaser and a joker and an almost frivolous young fellow, who in other times and in another country would have been a bullfighter scarred but not scared, a fast-moving racing-car driver or a happy-go-lucky playboy. Because of all that, this is not a photograph, but rather that *rara avis:* the image of the dead hero when alive.

THE FRENCH PHILOSOPHER AND HIS CONSTANT COMPANION visited with the comandante who ruled over the region. All the comandantes were in fact war lords. He was a tall man with a long rebel beard but wore his hair short. He had a face at once determined and benign. His complexion was dark but his eyes were 'blue like blue marbles' according to the philosopher who was hopelessly cross-eyed. The French woman said in what was meant as a whisper but came out as a sigh: *'Comme il est beau!'* Anyone could see that she wanted to fuck him *sur place*. But the philosopher was absolutely unconcerned and the comandante didn't understand French, not even French sighs or French whispers. What the Frenchwoman didn't know was that the comandante didn't care for sex, only for power. He took off his wide-brimmed stetson and placed it on the old sofa where he slept. Obviously he was not superstitious or perhaps he thought that the superstition of a hat on a bed as a bad omen did not apply to sofas. He invited the woman and the philosopher and their interpreter of course to have coffee. Then he sat down in his *taurete*, which is a chair covered with rawhide favoured by Cuban peasants.

He seemed at ease in his humble surroundings, as he did not care for comfort. The philosopher, who was a shifty thinker, wanted to know about the ideology of the revolution applied to an old colonial city like Trinidad. He called it Trinité but the interpreter got it right. 'I don't see any ideology in this town,' said the comandante who was less than a major but more than a mayor. 'I only see problems of war in peacetime. There are the problems of the city and the problems of the countryside: the land, the peasants. If you want ideology you'd better go back to

Havana.' The Frenchwoman, who was also a writer, wanted to know about Trinidad (she got it right), so old and beautiful a city and yet so dilapidated. The interpreter got it wrong and translated it as *dilapidación*, which means in Spanish the squandering of a fortune. Who knows what the comandante thought (public funds? his family's inheritance?) but he became angry or uncomfortable and he was about to stand up with extreme finality. But the interpreter, redressing his gaffe, told him that the writer only meant that the city seemed to be coming apart. 'That's a problem for architects,' said the comandante as he disclosed that he was a proud man. 'My sole concern is the population, who are fed up with living in derelict houses and walking on rough stones. It's not easy to live among the ruins.' He stood up now and they all did the same. The French philosopher looking crossed daggers at the comandante and the French lady still eyeing the tall, lean chieftain as she left.

Six months later a peasant revolt against the revolutionary government erupted all over the mountains and the comandante joined the peasants, a rebel twice over. They were all caught. Most of the peasants were relocated in remote areas of the island and all the chiefs of the rebellion were condemned without trial and massacred. The comandante was shot *sur place*. Before facing the firing squad as an utter defilement they shaved off his beard. But he still had eyes like blue marbles.

Years later, when the French lady writer published her memoirs of her visit to the paradise island, she mentioned the interpreter but she forgot all about the comandante.

WHEN HE WAS A WAITER he'd keep a gun in his locker in case some big boss from the regime (those were his words), or secret-service colonel or cabinet minister would come there to eat. Later he participated in the attack on a radio station the day they stormed the presidential palace. His cousin was with him. They survived the raid and were hiding together for a few days. Then they separated and he went to hide in the more dangerous place, while his cousin went to take refuge in a secure apartment. As one of the many ironies of guerrilla warfare, the secure place was raided by the police and they killed his cousin, while he lived to see the revolution triumph. They made him comandante, but having nothing to do, he got bored and collected weapons and ammunition in his house. One day he had a fight with his wife and set their double bed, under which he'd been keeping the ammunition, on fire. The explosions drew the attention of half the city and when he came out of the smoke, laughing, they detained him and stripped him of his rank. He was in prison for some time but then they let him go, eventually restored him to the rank of captain, and assigned him to the Ministry of the Interior, in charge of interrogating political prisoners.

A bachelor again, he now lived in a requisitioned house, or rather mansion, where he had a grand piano in the living room and a carpeted, cushioned room in the back for listening to and making music, since he was an amateur percussionist and played the drums very well. He also had a vast wardrobe (he'd change shirts several times in one night) and a collection of expensive cameras. He was always surrounded by a gang of people, and with his lean physique he looked like a bullfighter. Sometimes he had parties in his house, drinking with his friends and listening to jazz records and making music.

These parties lasted from midnight till four or five in the morning, when he'd go off to do his interrogation work. There was a method to his work. He would invariably take off his shirt to interrogate his prisoner and as the morning progressed and the heat of the cell made him sweat, he'd rub his armpits and make little balls with the sweat and dirt from his armpit. Then he'd throw these vile balls like bullets at the prisoner's face. He was considered an excellent interrogator, so much so that in a few months' time he again became comandante.

HE WAS THE MILDEST OF TERRORISTS until he was caught by the most vicious policeman the dictatorship had. He was tortured and almost killed and he swore revenge if he ever came out of the ordeal alive. As the dictatorship was discontinuous he was released some time later. Somehow he learnt the name of the policeman who so exclusively tortured him (the political police was always tremendously personal) and knew he was a colonel famous for his cruelty and his painstaking attention to detail in torturing. He bided his time and when the regime was overthrown he tenaciously looked for the colonel, *his* policeman, among the prisoners. He wasn't among them. A big shot, so to speak, he had escaped with the dictator, the chief of staff of the army, the chief of police and the rest of them. It was an exodus more than a retreat and only the foolhardy and the very brave stayed behind. Those were caught, tried and shot. But never at dawn: that's for the movies only. The mild terrorist was disappointed but he was still young. He could wait. He knew that sooner or later he was going to meet with his captor again. He felt like a character in Poe and he was comforted. Montresor had exacted his revenge from Fortunato after all. His memory would be his cask of amontillado.

The mild terrorist who was also a Catholic became a seasoned terrorist when he opposed the new regime – which for him was very like the old regime only worse. He had to flee the country for his life. Though he didn't leave as his torturer did, it was an exodus again.

Many years passed and he stopped being a Catholic and lived on a neighbouring island that looked very much like his native soil. He was still a mild man but never forgot the name of the henchman who tortured him: torture always leaves thick scars. He often wondered where he might live now.

One day, almost twenty years later, living in a city that looked like the Havana of lore, he was about to cross a busy thoroughfare that was known to be murder for pedestrians, when he saw an old man holding a white cane about to cross the street too. He shouted at the man to stand still. He then ran to him to tell him, 'Let me help you. This is a killing street, you know that.' But the old man didn't know.

He helped the blind man and when they had negotiated the dangerous crossing the old man thanked him and said, 'So you're Cuban too?' The younger man said yes. 'Do I know you?' The younger man said he didn't think so. 'But surely you know me,' said the blind man. 'My name's Carratala.' That was the name of the torturer he had been looking for for more than a quarter of a century. Carratala: somehow he had been looking for a younger man. What should he do? This man said who he was now, but was he the same man who had tortured him a long time ago and in another country? Had he read what Poe really said on the subject of revenge when he wrote: 'Villains do not always . . . meet with punishment . . . in reality?' Vengeance was his now at last. All he had to do was to take the old man back to where he found him or simply leave him in the middle of the road. But the younger man simply said: 'I've heard the name' – and went about minding his own business, which had nothing to do with politics or revolt or murder considered as a form of justice.

THE HOUSEWIVES CAME OUT, beating their pots and pans and shouting: 'We want food!' The crowd marched towards the centre of town, towards the square where 'the national flag had first been unfurled'.

Twenty miles from there, in the provincial capital, the captain of the garrison, who was at the same time the governor of the province, ordered the tanks to advance upon the town.

It all ended in their surreptitiously sending food to the mutinous town, while the fearless officer who had confronted pots with tanks was sent as ambassador to a North African country – and since then he's been known as the Tinhorn Rommel.

IN THE EARLY DAYS they were law students together and they became lawyers together. Then they even shared a *bufete* which was only a dusty room in Old Havana and they both were poor for a time. Later they engaged in political dealings together and the older lawyer, he with the flashing teeth in all the photos, was his best friend's best man when he was married. But then when the younger lawyer became the leader of an armed assault against the army on the other extreme of the island, the older lawyer decided he couldn't follow him: his friend's feat was an illegal action. When the younger lawyer named himself as a guerrilla chief to do battle to the regime in the mountains, his friend remained in Havana. Then, when his friend won, he became a powerful man: much more than a prime minister and even more than a president. His old friend was uncommitted. When the younger lawyer was christened the Maximum Leader by his followers he couldn't care less. He believed that illegal power always engenders illegal laws.

One day the Maximum Leader met his old friend by chance and showed some surprise. He thought that his friend had left the island to become a political exile. But he vowed that he was happy to know he was still in Cuba. 'So many have left,' he complained. The Maximum Leader always complained of imaginary grievances: somehow somebody somewhere was always against him. But this time he was right. It was obvious that his old friend didn't love him any more. If he didn't love then he hated him. Two days later the older lawyer was detained and thrown in jail. Later they announced that he was going to be tried for treason, condemned and shot in the prison's yard. He asked to lead his own defence and during the trial the old

137

lawyer had not a fool for a client. He knew he was fighting for his life and he presented to the tribunal a brilliant case for the defence: he knew he was innocent. He was sentenced to twenty years of hard labour. But he was pleased with himself: he never thought he could be such a good lawyer.

In jail, with the passing of years, he knew he was no longer a young man and perhaps he missed the time when he was the partner in law of the man who threw him in prison. He was ill many times or perhaps jail was one long chronic illness. He lost most of the teeth he was proud of. He became an old man at forty-five. He believed he would die in jail but he never cried.

Once a group of penal lawyers paid a visit to his jail and just by chance they saw the old lawyer. They had known him as a young lawyer and were surprised at how much older he looked. Whatever happened to him? they wanted to know. The old lawyer stated the obvious: it was the jail in particular and jail in general. He pleaded his case. He was not the brilliant lawyer he was at his trial, he was in fact pathetic and the next best thing, he was convincing. The visiting lawyers promised to take his message to the Maximum Leader, who was even more maximum these days. They visited him in his new presidential palace (he was now a prime minister, commander-in-chief of the armed forces, secretary-general of the ruling party and president of the republic: he was in fact omnipotent) and, after many official dealings, they gave the Maximum Leader, comrade, with utmost respect, his old friend's message. It went like this: 'The prisoner, President, is now an old man and he knows for a fact that he could not serve his full sentence.' The Maximum Leader adopted the pose of a thinking man, a thoughtful man: in his musing he even looked a bit like Rodin's *Thinker*. He appeared to be pained, even chagrined. Now he spoke thus:

'Please go back and tell him from me to try and serve as many years as he can.'

It was Machiavelli who warned lesser men of the danger of being an intimate friend of a tyrant.

The older lawyer died in jail.

THE COMANDANTE GAVE HIM A STORY TO READ. In it a man would go into the bathroom and spend hours locked inside. The wife worried about what her husband was doing in the bathroom for such a long time. One day she decided to find out. She climbed out of the window and walked along the narrow ledge that went around the house. She slid up to the bathroom window and looked in. What she saw stunned her: her husband was sitting on the toilet and had a revolver in his hand with the barrel in his mouth. From time to time he took the barrel of the gun out of his mouth to lick it slowly like a lollipop.

He read the story and gave it back to its author without further comment or perhaps with an offhand comment. What makes the story particularly moving is the fact that its author, the comandante, committed suicide seven years later by shooting himself in the head. So as not to wake his wife, he wrapped the gun in a towel.

TOWARD THE END OF DECEMBER 1958 he had embarked from a port in Florida with a cargo of smuggled weapons. But the boat met up with a northwester when crossing the strait and they lost their way. It was found, adrift, a week later, in January 1959. Fear of the sea or of death had made him turn grey overnight, and what is almost worse, delivery of the cargo would have been a poor anti-climax to his adventures: the dictatorship had fallen six days before.

In 1960 he was in an uprising against the government in the hills of Escambray, but he was captured by a squad of the so-called Combat Patrol Against Bandits, summarily tried and shot within twenty-four hours. His hair was still white.

IT ALL BEGAN WHEN AN AMERICAN went out on the balcony of his hotel the day they attacked the presidential palace and a nervous soldier fired on him and killed him. His best friend swore that he would avenge that death and came to the island and became a guerrilla fighter, eventually reaching the rank of comandante. Afterwards, in peacetime, he became an expert at breeding bullfrogs. He got to breed the largest frogs on the island and this American was proud of his ability to breed bullfrogs.

But one day they stopped a truck that was carrying weapons for the counter-revolutionaries in the mountains near the bullfrog farm. This American was driving the truck. He was summarily tried and shot at 7 p.m. one day in 1961 – barely five years after they had killed his friend.

AMONG THE COUNTER-REVOLUTIONARIES who had just landed there was a black man. The Combat Patrol Against Bandits surrounded them as soon as they landed, and when the captain saw him, he shouted: *Cabrón!* and killed him right then and there. The other counter-revolutionaries were taken to the capital and put on trial, some being condemned to death, others receiving sentences of thirty, twenty and fifteen years in prison. But they killed the black man right then and there.

AS THEY MARCHED TOWARD THE WALL, they shouted: 'Long Live Christ the King! Long Live Christ the King!' and they continued shouting after they were lined up against the wall and they were still shouting when they were shot. The ironic twist is that the fort where they were imprisoned and shot was right across the bay from the Archbishop's Palace.

THERE ARE MANY STORIES ABOUT FUGITIVES. Many are horrible, others are unavoidably funny, like the one about the Chinaman who escapes in a washtub and is received by the exiles with cheers, but the Chinaman is reluctant to be considered a hero, repeating again and again: 'Rook! Heelo's de uddel one,' until they finally see the other Chinaman entering the bay, seated in a chamber-pot. But the truth is not a joke.

The truth is that between seven and ten thousand persons have died trying to escape. Some have been shot down by the guns on shore or by coast-guard boats, others have been shipwrecked or drowned, many others have been eaten by sharks and many more dragged by the Gulf Stream until they've been wrecked in the middle of the ocean or annihilated by the rigours of nature, which doesn't differentiate between a good and a bad cause.

WE LEFT FROM A PLACE ON SANTA FE BEACH. In a raft made
of planks and car tyres. I remember that in the midst of
the uncertainty when we left, the doctor's mother took a
little dog with her and it started to bark. It's as if I can
now see them all again at the moment we left the shore.
She was the liveliest of all, at the same time trying to keep
the dog quiet. We all picked and occupied a place in the
raft. And we took off, since it was a good, moonless night.
For food we brought along some cans of condensed milk,
getting which had been harder than making the raft, and
also water and crackers. That's all.

Yesterday I was asked if I believed in God. I'm going to
tell you something. I had been missing something in my
life and that something I think I've achieved with this
great proof God has given me by letting me live to tell the
world about the voyage we had to endure in the midst of
a burning sun and that black sea.

The days passed and as they passed our raft started to
fall apart. How far we were from knowing what its end
would be! A mere sign from a boat or a plane would have
told us that we had been spotted . . . An uneasiness began
to take hold of us all. We had to restrict the intake of food
and water . . . Still there were hopes. But the days kept
passing, increasing everyone's desperation even more . . .
And then came the moment we had all feared so much:
the raft broke. Before, during the day, when it wasn't the
sun it was the waves, which made us grab on to the raft
so as not to fall overboard . . . At night the cold had made
us cuddle up against each other and put on the driest
clothes we had . . . When the raft came apart each one
grabbed a tyre or one of the planks. Whatever we could.
We had to cling to something to survive . . .

146

The rest of the group had been separated from us by the waves. During the first moments we saw them at a distance. Night closed in on us. Our small group tried to close the circle as much as possible, using the remains of the raft and the rest of the tyres. When dawn came we were surrounded almost immediately by a thick fog . . . You couldn't see anything. Suddenly I felt someone pulling hard on my clothes. It was the doctor, saying: 'I think my time has come . . . I can't get up any more strength . . . I'm sinking minute by minute . . . I try to hold on but I have no strength . . . I only ask you one favour: save my mother, save her . . . Please God . . . save her . . . save her,' and the doctor began to disappear little by little in the midst of that gentle mist.

Then I saw that the days and the nights were passing and I was still alive, drinking sea water and putting my head in the water, as long as I could, to refresh my burning face . . . But I was sure that I wasn't going to perish . . . It was like the end of a novel, horrible. Someone had to remain behind to tell the story. And I got it into my head that that someone was me. That idea accompanied me the rest of those days in which I had to stay in the sea, until an American fisherman picked me up . . . How did he do it? I can't explain. I was unconscious and the only thing I remember is that I think I asked the fisherman not to take me back to the island . . . What I do remember perfectly is that when I was the last one left I grabbed one of the tyres and put it around me to cover my backside, where I had received several fish bites, the kind of fish that can sniff blood. They did something similar to my thighs. See?

WHEN THE PLANE LANDED three thousand miles and eight hours later, a semi-frozen ball fell from between the wheels. He was the lucky stowaway. The red light that had lit up on the landing-gear controls was the unlucky stowaway. He was killed falling into the sea or on some deserted part of the island that they both had wanted to leave at all costs.

FIRST THEY TOOK MY LITTLE THEATRE AWAY FROM ME. You know, I had paid for it in instalments with my typist's salary from the railroad. They took it away. I arrived when they had already put the requisition stamp on the door and they didn't even let me take out my personal belongings. And for what? For nothing. Because they didn't even open it to the public any more. They simply took it away when nationalization came along and they closed it and left it like that, to rot. That's when I decided to leave the country. I requested a visa and from the very first paper, the first form I filled out, they took away my job and sent me to a labour camp. I was there a year and a half and the reason I didn't stay longer was that I got sick. I got an infection in my leg which spread from my thigh to my ankle. This I got from sleeping on the floor. They'd wake me up at the crack of dawn and take us to a nearby field to cut sugar cane and then a little further away to plant arum and eucalyptus trees. And we were in the fields until nightfall, when we'd return to the sheds and collapse on the floor, and there would be times when we'd have to push the rats aside to make a place. I don't know what those rats did inside the sheds, because there was more to eat outside on the ground than inside there. We got so hungry that the other prisoners began to hunt lizards and birds for survival. But I couldn't do that. They even killed a crow and ate it raw, almost with its feathers on. But I could never kill a bird or a lizard to eat and I got very weak working there. That's what saved me. From being so poorly fed I got that infection and the camp bosses decided to send me home for fear that they would catch it.

149

ONE DAY IN MAY 1965 the Cuban cultural attaché in London received orders in code from the ministry to make himself available as an interpreter for an official from the Ministry of Foreign Trade. This was not unusual but what followed was very unusual. Both visit and business were to remain strictly confidential. Nobody else at the embassy, except for the ambassador and the agent from G2 (who doubled as decoder), should know the content of the cable. The very morning the trade official arrived the cultural attaché went with him to a well-known steel firm in Essex. The manager was a middle-aged man who covered his bald patch with lank hair that visibly belonged to the other side of his head. He was eager to do business and greeted his prospective customers with a smile so wide that his false gums, not to mention his teeth, showed. The attaché explained that his colleague had been sent by their Government to buy barb wire. Barbed wire, he corrected himself. The attaché had been educated in the United States and he was concerned that somehow it always showed in England. He was worried that it might show in Cuba. The English merchant, who knew how to make a kill, wanted to know the exact amount of wire required. The man from Havana quoted a figure and the merchant excused himself before he delved into some calculations. Some time later he lifted his cherubic face from his figures to say in jest: 'Why gentlemen, that's barbed wire enough to fence in the whole island!' The cultural attaché translated the remark to his colleague and the man from Havana said in Spanish: 'That's the general idea – but don't interpret it.'

IN A FEARFUL SYMMETRY concentration camps mushroomed again all over the island around 1966. But the barbed wire was painted pink this time. The electrified fences were erected to concentrate homosexuals only. They were arrested *en masse* in cities and towns mostly, under a new law called the Improper Conduct Act. No congress worthy of that name would approve it. Apparently improper conduct meant that, though sent to do hard labour, the inmates were not to be considered counter-revolutionaries, maladjusted citizens or common criminals. They were simply guilty of improper conduct, even if they had committed no other crime. There were no courts to try them properly or a jury to agree on a verdict. Unrecorded sentences did not specify any lengths of time in jail but they always came before the verdict. The Improper Conduct police were in fact sole prosecutors and judges as they carried out orders issued directly from above. Yet nobody could say precisely what kind of crime it was 'to behave with improper conduct'. Thousands of citizens, many of them artists and writers, were condemned by special decree 'without regard to individual culpability'. Nobody knew what the crime was but it seemed at the time that it was something inherent, like being a Jew in Germany around 1936. The country, it is true, was poor in Jews but rich in *maricones, patos, pájaros, cundangos, locas* and *pederastas:* the nomenclator's paradise. If the culprits tried to find out what improper conduct was they would eventually discover that by just doing so they became guilty of improper conduct.

Finally the prisoners were confined with extreme prejudice in several concentration camps built on remote sites on the island. The camps were a well-kept secret for a while, but as with most secrets it was discovered eventually. When this happened nobody came forward to assume responsibility. Some high-ranking officials said they didn't even know that there were concentration camps on the island. Others maintained that they had never heard the phrase 'Improper Conduct' before. A minister for Culture, whose ministry had been particularly stricken by the malady, questioned by the press in Spain, swore that 'Improper Conduct' was an infernal invention of the enemies of the Revolution living in exile and abetted by the media. Interviewed by an American journalist, the Maximum Leader claimed that *improper conduct* did not belong 'in our vocabulary'. He used to call the enemies of the people names like worms, chancres and because they lived mostly in the US, cold sores. But not any more. 'As to the camps,' he avowed, 'yes, they existed but they're all in the past now. Why speak of the past in a country of the future?' The journalist then asked him about his cows. 'They're not my cows,' said El Maximo. 'They belong to the people. I'm only the veterinarian.'

THERE WAS AN UGLY AND ROUGH DIPLOMATIC COURIER who loved tangos. When he came to London he always asked to be taken to an Argentine watering hole in Soho where they played tangos after dark. He was a sentimental courier and he wept easily. He usually stayed in the bar until the wee hours to have a weep with every tango. But it takes two even to listen to a tango. As it was the duty of the cultural attaché to be present at all cultural functions, he had to take the weeping courier to Soho though he hated it. The diplomatic courier also loved to drink and get drunk and cry. He did all of that that fateful night.

The morning after and without the trace of a hangover he went straight to the ambassador (couriers had many prerogatives) to accuse the cultural attaché of being a *maricón*, which is the worst kind of paederast in Spanish. The courier swore before the flag of the Revolution (it was a tiny one on the desk of the ambassador) that the comrade attaché had made a pass at him while being drunk and then softly tried to open his fly, which luckily was buttoned up and not zippered. Perhaps the attaché had thought that in Communism private parts cease to be private. Or perhaps the courier had had one tango too many. Or he was lying. In any case the cultural attaché was recalled to Havana, dismissed from the Foreign Office and sent to one of the Military Units Helping with the Agriculture, also called UMAP, accused of improper conduct abroad. UMAP is how the concentration camps were named in the official jargon. The camp in which the cultural attaché was interned had a sign high above the gate which said: 'ONLY HARD WORK WILL MAKE MEN OF YOU.' They say the attaché wept before it.

153

HE WAS STATE PRISONER Number 2717 and he had been put in isolation in the maximum-security sector of the Castillo del Príncipe. He had been a student leader who had fought in the underground against the previous regime and now he was imprisoned, as before, for 'conspiring against the powers of the state'. He was tried and sentenced to ten years of prison in 1960, but he was still in prison in 1972. At first they put him in the circular penitentiary on the Isle of Pines, but when he tried to escape from there they stopped him with a bullet that left him semi-paralysed. Now he weighed only eighty-five pounds and he looked like a living corpse. He argued with his captors to the end, and once or twice he went on a hunger strike. When he died he was buried secretly and they didn't notify his relatives and they refused to give his body to his mother when she found out about it days later.

I CAN'T WRITE . . . My God, I'm a total wreck. Maybe later. Tell them that this is a suffering I have to bear, but what they've done to him is beyond words. I'm telling you . . . the day before yesterday when we went to the cemetery we were followed by patrol cars and all, can you imagine, we were quiet and respectful and almost three hundred soldiers and two hundred patrol cars blocked our way – just think, even after death they're afraid of him. Go tell the free world, if such a thing exists – because nothing exists! Can you imagine . . . I called and told them my son was dying for his country; some country – shit! Where are those human rights they're all talking about? The most terrible thing, that's what they did! Can you imagine, they bury him and three days later they come to tell me . . . No, I'm sorry, no, no, *no, no, no!* There are no words for what they've done! I fought for twelve years to save my son and he died like a dog, I didn't even know where he was . . . they didn't even want to tell me where he was, where he was buried. Did you know that I was in prison, they had me there . . . They did horrible things to me, those bastards. This is the life . . . this the freedom we have in this country . . . Not a single voice was raised, nothing was said, nobody said a thing to get them to give him medical care – shit – which nobody should be deprived of . . . Oh, yes, they all knew! . . . But nobody did anything! Even the Pope . . . What good has it done me to be such a good Catholic? . . . And to have such a noble son as he was, because never has there been a Cuban, the God's honest truth, who has sacrificed himself for this country so that . . . What they've done to him is beyond words . . . Can you imagine, after burying him they had me going around in a hundred circles before they

155

told me. I didn't think they were such cowards! . . . The most cowardly thing there ever was . . . You know that the day before yesterday me and twelve other women went to bring wreaths . . . and from behind the tomb-stones a mob of over three hundred thugs jumped out on us . . . You should only know what it is to be a desperate mother like me, alone in this shitty world, where nobody listens to me . . . I got tired of phoning and telling the whole world: For the sake of humanity, do something! . . . But nobody . . . Where? Here or there? Because they told me he didn't get medical care . . . And like a dog I was, climbing up those steps of the Castillo del Príncipe. Those bastards, it shouldn't happen to anyone . . . I was in the prison even . . . They brought three doctors to me after they killed my son . . . because what they put me through was terrible . . . They even beat me, those bastards! There are no words for our suffering . . . What a man he was! Ay, I don't think they did anything for my poor son there. Forty-five days without medical care! They set the mattresses, the beds, on fire, his fellow prisoners set everything on fire crying for help – shit – and nobody brought help . . . Oh . . . they know that, do they? Some great organizations . . . the Red Cross, you say? But did they do something? He died like a man! He died for Cuba! He died for his fellow prisoners! . . . Something nobody ever does for them – because this is the greatest loss I've ever had – they should say Mass for him . . . they should let the world know what this is . . . Do you know what it is to deny a mother her own son's body? . . . Do you know what it is not to know how he died . . . You know how they persecute people. I went to bring him flowers. When I did, a mob of like two hundred thugs came after me. They didn't do anything. They didn't move an inch. They came here looking for me. I had to throw them out of this house . . . I'm demanding a firing squad, I am –

let them take me to the wall. They've killed my son! I'm
telling you, they took him away from me . . . They've
killed him, my son . . . they've killed him . . . Ay, that
man was an example to the world. And I don't even know
how my son died . . . Can you imagine that yesterday,
the day before yesterday, me and twelve women, sad
women, relatives of the prisoners . . . Because they didn't
give his body out of fear, because they were afraid the
people would rise up. They didn't give him up out of fear,
because they were afraid of him even after he was dead.
Because I want you to know . . . the order was from higher
up . . . The order was that he had to be eliminated. There
was nothing to be done! People have to speak up, they
have to make those human rights people see that many
prisoners are still walled up, they have to see what they
can do for them – shit . . . Because they're dying – shit!
Shit – because they're dying! They have to make a move
on that issue, you know, because there are many here . . .
I'm going to keep fighting! Because those prisoners were
his brothers . . . Thank you very much, but please do it
for those who are still there, because he died for his fellow
prisoners . . . Human Rights . . . that International Red
Cross . . . that OAS . . . those figureheads . . . While
these poor people are dying like flies in the prisons, those
bastards! You should see what the Boniato prison's
like! . . . You should see how they look when they come
out of there . . . And I'll stay here, I won't move from
here because they're fighting, the same as my son . . . No,
my other son doesn't need me. He should be happy not
to be here, because he would have been in prison
already . . . No, no, impossible, they didn't let me take
any calls . . . I don't even know how you got through. Up
until now they haven't said anything about him being
dead and it's already been eight days . . . Tell them that
he died like a man . . . because he died for his brothers

who are in prison and he died for his Cuba – shit! Yes . . .
go to Mass . . . tell them to say Mass and to keep talking
and talking and fighting for those who are still here,
because there are still thousands of prisoners here . . .
Now they've toned it down a bit because a real man has
died, but in a little while they'll be back at it again. They're
dying walled up in Boniato – shit – and nobody's doing
nothing for them. Nothing . . . I'm telling you, I'll still be
here right with them, to die beside them and to be reunited
with my son again . . . And what goes on here are people
who come to spy on me and watch me and when it's not
a patrol car it's something else. That night over eight patrol
cars came when I didn't have my poor son at my side . . .
The next day they informed me that my son was dead,
those bastards. What can you do if that thug's the biggest
murderer Cuba has ever had? Tell them that I'll die right
here . . . with the prisoners . . . When they told me: Pedro
Luis Boitel is buried, he's already buried . . . To say that
to a mother . . . And they took me prisoner and beat me
and everything . . . No . . . No . . . No, just imagine, they
themselves admit that they made the biggest mistake in
their life! But he's dead! He's dead already! His cellmates
set the mattresses on fire, tore the beds apart protesting
for them to give him, for them to give him medical care,
those bastards . . . (*Here the call is cut off.*)

AND IT WILL ALWAYS BE THERE. As someone once said, that long, sad, unfortunate island will be there after the last Indian and after the last Spaniard and after the last African and after the last American and after the last Russian and after the last of the Cubans, surviving all disasters, eternally washed over by the Gulf Stream: beautiful and green, undying, eternal.

Index of first lines